SURPRISE

ENCOUNTERS

FOR LITERARY HEAT

www.BarbarianSpy.com

This book is copyright © Sabb 2012
Sabb asserts his right to be known as the author of this work
Published by BarbarianSpy in 2015
Cover design by BarbarianSpy © 2015
Cover Photo © Josetandem @ Dreamstime.com
All rights reserved.
Ebook ISBN 978-1-921879-36-4
Paperback ISBN: 978-1-925190-53-3

BarbarianSpy
Toronto
Australia

SURPRISE

ENCOUNTERS

an anthology

Sabb

TABLE OF CONTENTS

INTRODUCTION

I am not sure what to say to introduce this collection of twenty-four short stories to you. None involves a motor mechanic, but one involves miners. They all involve surprises, but some are surprises that occur in relationships and some are surprise sexual encounters with strangers. Most are meant to be nothing but entertaining, yet a couple are very serious. Some were first written to entertain "him," the man I most want to entertain and who inspires me as no one else does, and a few were not. Several appear in our Shabbu collections.

I think the best I can say for these is "may you enjoy reading them as much as I enjoyed them when I wrote them."

Sabb

5,000 WORDS BY 5 PM

Ranklestein chomped on his cigar and sucked smoke into his lungs as he stared at the text on the laptop. "Fuck. What a boring piece of . . . of boring crap."

The buzzing of the phone jerked him away from his typing. "Hi," he barked.

"Hi. So how's it going? I need those five thou by this afternoon, Rank. Five thousand; is that so hard?"

"Hard? Hard? This Manissus is a moaner and a wimp with the sex appeal of two-day-old road kill. Geez. I mean, who created this guy? You think I can work miracles in four hours?"

"It was Guy Royal's last heroic, erotic, action fantasy, OK? He was dying of pancreatic cancer, the most painful, Rank, baby, hear that? And his agent had just run off with his boyfriend, and he was almost destitute, for god's sake. If it hadn't been for guys like Brad, he'd have . . .ugh, well . . . he'd have starved. And you expect him to be cheerful? Feeling sexy? Hey, get real. Anyway, Guy Royal was a star. A cult figure. *Battle of the Gods* will sell whatever kind of shit it is. You I am paying to make it raunchy without making it unrecognizable, OK? Fifty thousand sexed-up words by the end of the month, but I need those five thou today, baby."

"Geez, Sol, if I didn't have alimony to pay, I'd say go fuck yourself."

"See. I knew you could do it, baby. So, by 5:00 PM? OK?"

"OK. OK, all right," Ranklestein barked and slammed down the phone.

"Shit," he added, chomping down grimly on his cigar and returning to reading the first chapter of *Battle of the Gods*, the gay epic that had been recovered from the late Guy Royal's hard drive after his death. A miracle, everyone was calling it. "Another tidy earner they can all live off for a few years till they find another Royal," Rank grumbled, "Christ. I wish they'd buried it with him."

He was reading again.

> *Fortunately for the man Manissus, the moon was nearly full, and even more fortunately, the goddess' bright silver face was sitting almost directly overhead in a clear night sky. A sky that was typical in that year of dry weather that had been frustrating the region's farmers throughout the mild winter, and looked like continuing into the approaching spring.*
>
> *The brightness of the night was a fortunate gift from the goddess, because otherwise Manissus would have fallen often as he made his way drunkenly through the narrow, unevenly paved streets of the city.*

Unfortunately, as far as Rank was concerned, the story was no gift from anyone and continued in the same woefully depressing, long-winded way for quite a few pages before there was even a hint of sword action of either the violent kind or the male/male sex kind.

"Moan, moan. Christ, if he didn't get any, then whose fault was it?" Rank asked out loud as he read on in exasperation, seeing all the missed opportunities for hot action.

> *It had been far from the intimate evening Manissus had hoped for and needed. Instead, Thesis seemed to have invited all the men of his family along to the dinner party, and it had already been far too late when the last of them had departed. Manissus should have left then himself, but he had waited impatiently all evening to be alone with his friend. Then when he was the only one left, Manissus had finally staggered over to join Thesis on his couch, believing that the evening would be worth it after all. But Thesis had sat up just as he reached him, wished Manissus a safe journey home, and made his excuses.*

"A hunky Greek from the time of the Trojan wars, and all he could do was stagger over and whine when he didn't get any. Geez. I mean, just throw this guy Thesis back on his couch and take his dick in your mouth, and he'd be begging for it after thirty seconds. Guaranteed," Rank shouted as he pulled his own cock free of his pants and gave it a stroke, imagining the two ancient Greeks dropping their linen whatevers and getting naked together on the couch. "Or an orgy. Yeah, the whole damned lot of them. All those relatives he invited along. Oh yeah," a hard-on always helped him think of sex to put in a story. "Hey Brad," he called out between pants. "Come out here."

His houseboy, Brad, padded out to the poolside patio wearing nothing but a thong and an all-over tan.

"Yes? You called, master?" Brad joked, striking a hand-on-hip pose and making his abs bunch up and his arms and legs flex, a blond, bronzed god with the oversized swimming pool in the background.

Now, there was a real Greek god, thought Rank. "Oh yeah, you look so good. But I've got a problem, babe.

I need inspiration; I need somewhere to start with this Guy Royal thing. Forget hot sex even. I need anything. It's dead. Like buried." He stuck his cigar back in his mouth and sucked briefly, while taking in what Brad had to offer and stroking himself a bit more quickly.

"I mean this guy is such a bore. You have read this. So, give me inspiration."

Brad frowned. "I liked it; I thought it was very literary, very artistic."

"Literary? Royal wasn't about literary, babe. Royal's all about sword action. Both kinds. I like the café bit, when he sees the hot young guy his ex-buddy Thesis is drooling all over now."

"That bit? That's hot?" Brad asked pouting. "He discovers his buddy, the man he loves, is chasing some eighteen year old. It's a pivotal emotional moment," he argued.

It was Rank's turn to frown. "Yeah? Pivotal?" he shrugged. "Well, I could see real potential there. Great three-way building. But it's way into the story. There's potential before that. And Sol wants the first five thousand words by 5:00 PM, and hot."

"You'll come up with something," Brad replied huffily, then moved in behind Rank and rubbed his crotch against Rank's upper back, making his employer close his eyes and his head flop about from side to side as he emitted small moans. "Just as long as you don't change the story," Brad said firmly.

"Yeah, the story's got lots of possibilities. Oh, yeah, now that's inspiring," Rank murmured, as he grabbed Brad's arm and pulled him around so he could tug off the thong and wrap a hand around the sausage it had been trying to hide. Brad bent over and they kissed, as the houseboy's hand joined his employer's on Rank's rock-hard very thick, six-and-a-quarter-incher.

"Start with yourself, baby," Brad said as he kicked off the thong and pulled Rank's hand free of his stiffening meat. "I'll be back in two shakes," he added reassuringly as he padded back into the low-set, white-painted, Spanish-style house.

"OK. So . . ." Rank returned his attention to his laptop.

> *Then, when he was the only one left, Manissus had finally staggered over to join Thesis on his couch, believing that the evening would be worth it after all.*

"De dah, deh, dah-now . . . ," Rank mumbled and started to type.

> *Manissus knelt by his friend's couch and grasped Thesis' organ through the fine linen fabric of his short tunic and felt it stiffening instantly. He stroked it lovingly; he had been waiting all evening, for Thesis's cock to be rock hard and throbbing. Now he was shaping the fabric around it, feeling it engorging under his attentions, and then, as it grew longer he was licking it, making the fabric transparent . . .*

Brad came padding back with a fistful of condoms and a tube of lube, and Rank looked up at him. "This has potential, loads of it. . . . But, shit, he just lets it drift by. I mean Royal was good. Well, I read him once, and it was real hot and heavy. This . . . this ain't Royal; it's . . ."

Rank paged forward,

> *. . . a line of men burned the color of cedar by days spent laboring naked, or almost so, under the hot sun, were passing up and down the two gangplanks running from the ship's side to the new stone dock.*

"There's more potential there too," Rank mumbled. "Lines of naked men, sweaty and muscular, I mean . . . When you were visiting Guy, did he ever talk about this *Battle of the Gods?*" Rank asked, frowning and taking a puff on his cigar.

"I think he mentioned something about it. About it being real literature," Brad replied sharply, seeing that Rank had an idea he wasn't going to let go of. "But I don't really remember."

And Rank's thoughts were interrupted just then as Brad's now well-filled tool was pushed at his lips, and he opened automatically to take in and suck his favorite treat.

For several minutes the only noises were Brad's grunts and moans and the sound of Rank's sucking and slobbering on Brad's rock-hard eight inches of cock. Rank always almost choked on it before he got the deep-throating action right, and then it was a smooth head-pumping face fuck that had them both moving on to another plane. And once the action was right, Brad held Rank's head in his hands, guiding it, and as the tension inside him built up, he rolled the middle-aged graying head from side to side as he pushed it back and forth. Brad loved the moving pressure Rank's mouth provided for him, like another kind of all-over stroking action.

Rank's cigar was sitting in the ashtray beside his laptop and went out about the time Brad decided he would come if he kept doing what he was doing. And he didn't want to come just yet. Brad pulled his cock from the sucking mouth with a slurping sound, as Rank tried to hang on to it. He loved sucking cock—loved the feel of a cock in his mouth almost as much as he loved the feel of one inside his ass.

Brad gave him an open-mouthed kiss, playing his tongue about in the warm mouth that tasted slightly of him, and with his hands under his arms, lifted Rank up. Rank kicked off his own pants and pushed his briefs down and then pulled Brad's hips in tight to his so the two rock-hard cocks were rubbing against each other and sending Rank off into a whimpering sucking of Brad's tongue in his mouth.

Brad pulled free, and Rank cried, "Oh yes, I want your cock, baby, fuc . . ." the cry was cut off abruptly as Brad stuffed the dead cigar into Rank's mouth. The loud vocalizing during sex wasn't going down well with their new neighbors, and the police were always happy to come and investigate the complaints.

With his mouth now full of cigar, Rank was quiet as Brad turned him around, and Rank chomped down hard on the firmly rolled tobacco as he bent over and rested his elbows on the seat of his chair, stuck his butt up in the air, and widened his stance. He made grunting and mumbling noises as he looked back under his chest, back to what was going on between his spread thighs. His erection bounced up and down, revealing and then hiding his tight balls, and behind him he saw Brad's thighs. Brad moved in closer and inspected Rank's hole and briefly let himself imagine the different ways he could open it up.

He loved giving a good fuck just as much as Rank liked taking one, and his urge today made him stroke over that well-used puckered rim with the big red cap of his own tool, a sight he never tired of seeing. His cock head stroking up and down between the parted cheeks and over Rank's tightly puckered rim.

Rank grunted and moaned and whimpered as he chewed on his cigar before he finally had to reach back for his own dick and stroke himself to completion. He could never hang off like Brad could, and once he felt a cock at his rim, he was usually coming.

Some lube fingered into the slack hole, and Brad was guiding his big cockhead to it. Then, with the head barely in, he thrust hard. The cigar butt shot out of Rank's mouth as he let loose an almighty cry of "Yeeoww." Then he was shouting loud enough to be heard half a block away, as Brad started deep pumping him, "Fuck. You're fucking killing me. Ohh, I can't take it."

The cigar was too far away to be rescued, so Rank just continued yelling as Brad plowed his ass in a frenzy. The neighbors called the police and were yelling complaints over the fence at them at about the same time Rank got hard again. His cries took on a new pitch as he beat himself off and Brad lightly squeezed his balls, and his yell of "I'm coming. Coming, coming, coming" was indecipherable. Brad came with a small grunt and did the rotation of his hips that always made him moan it felt so good, and he rotated them again for another jolt.

Brad finally pulled out, satisfied, and Rank eased himself up and back into his seat and the two men kissed.

"Just as long as you don't change the story," Brad said firmly, before he retrieved his thong and carried it back into the house.

For a moment Rank sat there silently, still spent and mellow, but then he looked at his computer and finally focused. For a few minutes Rank read and pondered.

"He didn't write this," Ranklestein suddenly said, sitting bolt upright. "What is Sol baby trying to pull? Guy Royal never wrote this shit. I doubt he ever set eyes on it even." He frowned and skimmed a bit and then called, "Brad, here, baby."

Brad reappeared in a clean thong, carrying a fresh cigar, and wandered over to his employer. "You rang?" he said jokingly as he handed over the cigar.

"You were there in Royal's house. Just about every bloody day. So, Brad, spill. What's the story with this *Battle of the Gods*?" Rank asked, shoving the six inches of cheap machine-rolled tobacco into his mouth. "This ain't Royal's writing, and don't distract me again," he added, as Brad made a grab for Rank's dick and Rank batted his hand away.

"What was that thing you wrote for that creative writing course you did? The thing you never showed me? That was some ancient Greek story, wasn't it?"

Brad looked surprised, "But . . . you never listen to anything I say. All I am to you is a sex object."

"I always hear you," Rank argued. "You're hot as hell, but I listen babe. I swear. And what's wrong with being a sex object anyway?"

Brad sniffed, Brad pouted, Brad looked Rank in the eye and said reluctantly, "Guy liked it," and straightening up to his full six feet, he added, "He was going to help me knock it into shape and find a publisher. That's why it was in his computer." Then he crumpled up and his eyes went blurry. "Are you going to tell, Sol?"

Rank didn't even have to think about that. "Fuck, Sol. Far as he's concerned, this is Guy Royal's story. And if it's Guy Royal's, it will sell and we all get paid and everyone's happy. This has potential. I can make it raunchy. You didn't put anything else on his computer, did you? Leave any disks around someone could find? Anything like that? I mean Sol's desperate . . . and I can make anything hot . . ."

"No," replied Brad, huffily, "I slaved over that, Rank, and Guy said it was a work of art, real literature."

"Humph. Guy was dying, and you were feeding him, babe," Rank replied, patting Brad's ass. "I can tell you it ain't going nowhere as it is. But why no sex, baby? That's all it needs. It's got great openings, so many scenes that can be turned into strokes. So why, baby?"

"Because I wanted to prove that I can do more than just give a great fuck, Rank," Brad replied in anguish.

Now the truth was out Brad was wondering if it was time to stop arguing for *Battle of the Gods* to be left as it was, unraunchy and literary, but he'd already had ten rejections on it and was getting depressed. And he had some idea of what Guy's books had earned the old man. He was saved from further thinking by the bell, as just then he heard the door chimes and instead of arguing with Rank, he went to answer the front door. He knew who it was, so he greeted the two policemen by throwing the door wide and striking a hand-on-hip pose for them, his abs bunched up and his muscles flexed and a big smile on his face.

"And what can I do for you today, officers?" he asked.

* * * *

Three months later.

Ranklestein chomped on his cigar and sucked smoke into his lungs. "Fuck. What a boring piece of . . . of boring crap."

The buzzing of the phone jerked him away. "Hi," he barked.

"Hi. So how's it going? How's *Servant of the Great Moghul* going? Another week, Rank. OK?"

"OK. OK. It's boring shit, but I'm the great Rank. I can make anything raunchy, right, Sol? And how's *Battle of the Gods* selling?"

"Off the shelves, Rank. Still flying off the fucking shelves. Hottest thing Guy ever wrote. One hundred thousand copies local U.S. sales already," Sol replied. "And have you got anything else off those disks Guy gave Brad to keep safe for him?" he added in a wheedling voice.

"I reckon we can make something more out of them, Sol, baby. Couple of story outlines, and a few more disks to go through," Rank replied, leaning back in his chair and sucking contentedly on his cigar. "Yeah. A few more disks. Guy was sure prolific. And I reckon he started twice as many things as he finished, Sol. Yeah. Those disks of Brad's are a veritable gold mine. His lawyer's drawing up that contract, by the way."

"Hey, do we need a contract, Rank? I mean Brad's family," Sol exclaimed.

"Brad's not getting any younger, Sol. He's got to think of his old age. And if he's anyone's family, he's mine, Sol, baby. OK? So, ciao. I gotta go sex-up this crap." Rank cut the call.

Brad was seated on the other side of the patio table bent over his laptop, "So, how many books do you expect me to write?" Brad asked, looking over the top of his reading glasses at Rank. "And one day I want to be taken seriously as a writer, Rank. I'm not pumping out great historical novels for you to raunch up forever, you know," he added, pouting at his business partner.

"Sure, baby. But this will improve your writing, the more you write the better you get. And we can sell however many you can write, baby. So, how's the last chapter of *Servant of the Great Moghul* coming?" Rank asked.

Brad got up, naked except for his thong, and came around behind Rank and rubbed his mound over Rank's back. "You're distracting me, babe," Rank moaned as he put his cigar in the ashtray and turned around and flipped Brad's growing dick out of his thong and made love to it with his tongue. He probed the slit as the big cock hardened up and tasted the precum that the finger he had up Brad's ass was helping to make flow. He had a star to keep happy now, and he loved any excuse to suck cock, so there was no problem.

"Tongue around," Brad groaned and Rank obliged him, his tongue swirling about the head of Brad's cock. Then the cock was moving further into his mouth, moving down his throat and then out again. He gulped and sucked and took it all in again. Feeling the soft cap stroking his throat, the slick hardness, and tasting the salty taste. He tried to hang onto the big meaty piece as Brad pulled it free.

"Over," brad ordered and Rank obediently leant over the table and spread his cheeks and wiggled his butt as he widened his feet. "Give it to me. Give it to me, babe," Rank wailed loudly, as Brad dug a finger into his hole and found his prostate.

Then it was two fingers, and then three stretching Rank's ass. His groans and shouts got louder, and he couldn't hold back on stroking himself. Brad didn't bother sticking the half-smoked cigar in Rank's mouth. He quite enjoyed occasional visits from the local police, and it had been a while. Instead, he used his cock head to rim Ranks ass and then, positioning it at his entrance, drove it in with one great plunge.

"Yeooooowww," Rank cried as the thick eight-incher buried itself to the hilt inside him.

"You're killing me," he wailed, as Brad bottomed inside him, and his cries kept up as Brad fucked him slowly for a good twenty minutes, before coming, at the same time as Rank let loose his second load of cream.

After they had kissed Rank picked up his cigar and relit it.

"Guy Royal smoked cigars too." Brad observed. "Do you think I'd be taken more seriously as a writer if I smoked a cigar?"

"No," Rank replied sharply, "And stop distracting me. You haven't finished the last chapter, have you, babe? Have you even started it?"

Brad pouted and hearing the front door chimes, hurried off to answer, leaving Rank worrying about his deadline. No, their deadline, Rank realized, sighing and taking a long draw on his cigar.

A BOOK LOVER'S TALE

The humor was infectious.

Not that it was a funny book, just that the way the story was told tickled Grant just right. And he was, he realized belatedly, stroking himself off as he imagined fucking the book's hero, Robert. It was the tenth "Robert" book, the latest one, fresh off the press. Grant had only discovered them eighteen months before, so the time between then and now had been fairly well occupied by the ten novels.

Robert was a slightly offbeat cop who always arrived at the wrong time. And if the case got solved, it was because he got caught in the middle of some siege or chase or whatever where the bad guy confessed to him at the end of it. But Robert also worked out seriously, and was a bit of an amateur power-lifter who also sang in the local Methodist church choir.

The books had a steady cult following but were never likely to be best sellers. Grant knew that. They were a bit too literary, and a gay cop was also too way out for most readers. Not that Robert was very gay. Any sex he had was suggested to have occurred or hinted at, rather than graphically described. But that was fine with Grant. He had a very good imagination, and there was nothing like that sense of humor, which Robert's character was always written with, to make him happy. And nothing like Robert's way of talking about another man he was feeling hot for, to make Grant hot.

What really annoyed Grant now was knowing he'd have to wait at least six months for the next new Robert book to come out. But he hadn't finished this one yet and was taking his time. He could definitely imagine Robert lying back on the weight bench recovering his breath after pressing 150 kg for eight reps. Yep, and he just slid onto the bench between Robert's thighs and lifted his muscular legs and flipped his shorts off his butt and . . . yes. Robert was fucked—and was loving playing bottom to Grant's top. Though Grant knew Robert supposedly preferred to have things the other way round, and in the books he always did.

But Grant's gut feeling was that Robert would really like taking it. Hard and long and . . .

Yes, indeed. Grant pulled out a tissue and cleaned up.

Grant never went to gay events, he didn't even consider himself to be gay, or even bi—he was just, well, just getting a lot more male fantasy action and actual real action than the other kind of action nowadays. It was easier he rationalized, and there were fewer possible complications, and it was, well—good.

But Robert's creator, the author, Hamilton Sloan, was appearing at a gay literary event that Saturday. The thought of a gay literary event made Grant shudder, and part of him knew he shouldn't go. That part was sure the whole thing would be ghastly and that Hamilton, or whatever his real name was, would be some limp-wristed hairdresser type who Grant would take an instant dislike to. And taking a dislike to Robert's creator would, Grant knew, spoil Robert for him forevermore. And he didn't want to lose the good feelings he got from reading about Robert, or fucking him in his imagination.

But the other part of Grant couldn't not go. He was a man who accepted challenges. Well some challenges. And this Saturday was the first one in ages that he had free. It seemed like a sign. Grant could go, so he had to go. He sighed and read for a while longer before he finally set the book down for the evening. *The Evening Train* it was called, about a series of muggings and rapes on a Washington, D.C., commuter train, where all the victims were good-looking male office workers wearing suits and overcoats. A bit of a risky plotline, Grant thought, taking the gay thing into the crime itself. Hamilton hadn't done that before. Robert was gay, but the victims and the murderer were always straight.

Robert, of course, had nearly been raped himself one day, when he wore an overcoat and a suit to the investigations office, because he was meeting his rich elderly aunt Maud for lunch. The image of Robert squeezed between the two dark-haired muscular young men of uncertain ethnic background, and being groped, had been what had just helped Grant to be well satisfied. The second time that evening. He could well imagine them feeling Robert up, one pressed in behind him and rubbing his huge rod against Robert's butt as he held Robert's arms trapped behind him. The one in front, a big hand inside Robert's unzipped pants, playing with him while the other hand relieved him of his wallet.

At the next stop they had tried to maneuver Robert off the packed train into a space that was set back out of sight between two station buildings. Robert had used some martial arts skills to get away, though. In spite of the knife that had appeared. Of course, he had lost the two horse-hung muscular young studs as they leaped the station fence, like cats, and disappeared up an alleyway.

Grant had grunted in disappointment at the sexless ending to the erotically charged scene and had gone back a page to the paragraph just before Robert began his escape.

That paragraph had ended with, *"The youth behind him had Robert's arms pinned back painfully, as his companion, another dark-haired muscular and dangerous youth unzipped Robert's pants, pushed his hand in and grasped his manhood."*

"Yes," Grant hissed, imagining Robert's dick jumping free as his own just had. "Yes."

Grant's imagination was off and running. Now Louie, the dark-haired muscular stud standing in front of Robert was pulling out his own huge rod, and the cop gasped at the size of it. Louie docked the two cocks together and needed both hands to stroke them.

Robert arched back, turning his head to the side and moaning. But other lips found his, and Paulie, the stud behind him, had his tongue slipping between Robert's parted lips and into his mouth. Robert welcomed the invasion, closing his mind to anything except the feeling of what the two young men were doing to his body.

"Yes," Grant whimpered.

Paulie locked his arms in a tight embrace of Robert's chest, rubbing himself against his captive's firm bubble butt as his tongue showed its possession of his victim's mouth.

Louie stripped Robert's pants off, while letting Paulie know what Robert had.

"A lovely big, hard eight-inch cock," Louie growled, "This guy is really hung, Paulie."

Paulie could feel Robert's bare ass through his own pants and judged it was safe to let go with one hand and drop his pants, so his throbbing tool could find the heavenly tight passage it wanted to burrow into. Robert suddenly felt the head of Paulie's naked tool being stroked up and down his crack, and he moaned around its owner's tongue, letting him know they both wanted the same thing.

But Louie's fingers got in first, and Robert groaned his disappointment at not feeling the hard rod behind him making its way up into him. Louie was obviously enjoying this new activity though, and Robert tilted his pelvis and widened his legs to give him better access. The young mugger had long, thick fingers, and Robert's moans were no longer ones of regret for Paulie's cock, as Louie added another finger, but in appreciation of the stretching and fucking he was now receiving from three of those long, thick, strong fingers. Then Louie was doing a hand and mouth job on Robert's dripping cock. His tongue rimming the head and cleaning up the drips leaking from the slit as it tried to enter it.

Robert lifted his legs and draped them over Louie's shoulders as Louie continued to work him open. Then Louie was standing and Robert pulled free of Paulie's kiss to look down at the muscular young man between his thighs. Louie lifted Robert's legs, one by one, and set his feet up on the chain mesh fence before him, and Robert widened his feet on the wire, lifting his ass higher.

"You have a lovely hole, man," Louie crooned, teasing the brown twitching eye with his thumb pad.

Robert writhed and moaned as Louie leaned in to kiss and claim his mouth. Both his hands were now pulling Robert's cheeks apart, with the longest fingers of both hands sinking deep and pulling wide. Robert sucked Louie's tongue in the way his channel wanted to suck in Louie's big cock.

Behind him Paulie was grunting, "Hurry up, man, I wanna fuck him too. I am aching, man."

Robert wanted to tell them how much he agreed, but then he turned and Paulie had his mouth again, now deadening the noises Robert was making as Louie made a last preparation. Bending to wet down Robert's finger filled entrance before removing his thick fingers and replacing them with his cock. Louie's cock made the long journey inside slowly, Paulie's mouth covering Robert's groans and cries, as he was filled deeply. Louie came quickly but the brief powerful fucking still had Robert moaning happily. Then Louie released Robert's feet from the wire mesh of the fence, his cock leaving Robert's hole with a sloppy, sucking sound, as the cop's feet fell to the ground, after which he and Robert fell into a deep kiss

"Yes," grunted Grant, seeing it all. The two would-be muggers went completely wild for Robert, who was ready, no eager, for a wild fucking from both of them. Preferably with seconds.

Paulie growled and pushed Robert forward, breaking up the battle of tongues that had been going on between the cop and Louie. He positioned his cap at Robert's cum-lubed entrance and, with a twist to his piece, forced the full head in.

Paulie stretched Robert enough to make him cry, "No, no," as the thicker rod made room for itself. Paulie bottomed and waited for a few moments for Robert to accommodate him. Then he slowly pulled Robert's shoulders back up toward him, catching his thighs in between his and stepping his own feet together, pushing Robert's thighs closer together without losing any depth. Louie moved in to run his hands and mouth over the arched torso of the impaled and moaning cop.

A train came into the station, and the three of them froze as they were—Paulie's cock throbbing deep inside Robert's stretched ass, Louie covering his mouth and pressed tight against him. His hands up under Robert's shirt, pinching his nipples, giving Robert plenty to yelp about around Louie's buried tongue.

"Yes," Grant grunted and moaned, his cream shooting out, with the departing train, in its rush to escape the station. He gazed sightlessly at the page before him for a few minutes as he recovered.

So, Saturday it was, at the University Co-op Book Shop. Grant sighed unhappily as he got up and headed for the kitchen for a quick snack before he fell into bed.

The literary event didn't seem to have a schedule. Typical student-run shambles, Grant thought, looking about at the late-teen, early-twenty-something crowd of mainly lesbians, milling about loudly. He sighed and looked around gloomily. Now he'd come, he decided he might as well stay a while and see if Hamilton would appear, but he certainly wasn't standing round waiting with the crowd. Instead, he headed to the coffee shop up on the mezzanine floor, overlooking the nonacademic book section. Unfortunately, that was crowded too, and he looked around wondering if he should just go, deciding that if he couldn't get a seat in five minutes, he would. But there was a table to one side where a lone middle-aged male was sitting reading, and Grant took a chance and went over.

"Is it possible for me to share your table?" he asked politely.

The man looked up, frowning. "Sure, go ahead," he replied, and, that done, his eyes immediately returned to his book.

Grant ordered a coffee at the counter and returned.

The other man glanced up as Grant sat and asked, "Are you here for the event?"

"Yes," Grant replied, clearing his throat.

His addiction to Robert wasn't something he had confessed to anyone else, ever. After all, he wasn't gay and people might get the wrong idea.

"Yes," he repeated, stumped about what else to say.

The man returned his eyes to the book, *Stone Buildings of Victoria*.

"Hamilton. I came to see Hamilton Sloan," Grant felt he had to say something to explain his presence.

He didn't want the man to think he was there for the launch of the BDSM how to manual he had seen signs for everywhere, down below in the bookshop. He couldn't even make out what was going on in a couple of the poster shots and was sure he didn't want to know.

"Oh," the man glanced up. "Do you read that stuff?"

"Yes," Grant admitted, looking away. "Um. I like his humor," he added, looking back at his table companion and feeling that some further explanation was required. "I'm not gay," he added, "but I like good murder mysteries."

The man's eyes were green, Grant realized, and large. He was older than he looked too, Grant decided. Everything about him was neat and calm and there was something else about him that was wildly attractive.

"And you?" Grant asked.

"Um. Same," the man said.

Grant felt a strange tingling as he said, "Robert is a great character. Great sense of humor."

"Yes," the man replied, "But not a very good detective."

Grant was piqued at his mate Robert being criticized by a stranger. "He always finds the killer," he said gruffly.

"I think it's more a case of the killer finding him," the man replied, smiling.

Grant, who had been about to disagree strongly, just said, "Rubbish," and wondered what the story was with his table companion.

"Grant," he introduced himself.

"Andrew," the man replied, and they briefly grasped hands across the table.

"Coffee?" Grant asked, having noted his companion's cup sitting empty since he'd joined him.

Over a coffee they chatted some more, but Grant's mind was not entirely on the chat. He had been busy lately and now he was opposite an appealing man, and he was aware of being in the mood for something to happen. He also noticed a couple of young men who moved about the café of the bookshop. A couple were eye-catching for sure, but just then it was actually the mouth of his companion that was the sexiest thing in the room to him. The mouth, and the hands, and the straight but flexible back. Grant was getting hard under the table.

"I don't think this Hamilton guy is coming," Grant said. "How about we get out of here for a while. Have lunch," he said, trying to think of an excuse to go someplace where things could get more personal.

He rarely picked anyone up in public, and he usually didn't know the other man's name or want to. Now he wished he had some good line to use, other than "I want to fuck you, Andrew."

"I want to fuck you, Andrew," he said, accidentally, as they left the bookshop.

Andrew laughed and turned to look at him. "Pardon?"

Grant stepped in closer to Andrew, so he could say it properly without anyone else being able to hear. "I said, I'm glad I met you Andrew."

Andrew smiled at him lopsidedly. "Oh, I thought you said 'I want to fuck you, Andrew.'"

"Oh," Grant said, confused now and wanting to disappear into the ground, as Andrew slipped off his jacket and folded it over his arm.

Andrew had on a short-sleeved shirt, and his upper arms were thick with muscle—power-lifter arms.

"Robert, is a power-lifter," Grant said not able to take his eyes off his companion's thick biceps.

"Yes, he is. I prefer to write about things I know," Andrew replied, smiling.

Grant stopped, blushing, his mouth hanging open. "Hamilton, um . . . .Hamilton Sloan?"

"Probably," Andrew replied.

Unexpectedly, their mouths came together in a kiss.

A FANTASY

You have stood at the window behind the curtain as I've fucked you, one hand on your belly as you suck on my thumb, stifling your moans and cries. The few diners left below are oblivious of what is happening just above their heads.

You are unobserved now but want to be seen—not by the diners perhaps, but you are wanton in your need at this moment, and I wonder how I'll satisfy us both. The lunch-time wine is lubricating your lust. The door of the room stands open still. One of the young Turkish waiters pauses to look in, and I signal him to come in and join us.

He smiles, then turns and calls out, and pauses again before entering. I pull you back into the room; you have your audience now. You step slightly forward, wanting him to see my cock moving in and out of you. He watches me stroking your ass, grunting his approval as you turn to him, your eyes telling him everything, and he drops his pants, freeing his huge cock. It's already jumping, and he strokes it as he reaches his other hand to your cock.

Another waiter arrives, another young Turk, who laughs at what he sees. You need more attention now, and I turn you to the heavy table and you lie forward. Then I turn you on me till you are on your back. One Turk jumps up and kneels, straddling your head, feeding his big cock to you. You suck him busily as he watches me, and the other continues to watch me stroking in and out of you. He soon grasps your pole and strokes it in time with his own long, thin one, still watching.

They joke with each other in Turkish, make hand signals, and I sense what they may be joking about. I plant my hand back on your belly and withdraw from your passage.

The Turk holding your cock moves between your thighs and feeds himself into you as I bend to kiss your nipples and add my hand to the other young Turk's.

We quickly have you spouting your seed for us. The young Turks talk, and the one you are feeding on pulls free and moves forward. He obviously wants to fuck you too. I wonder what they will do, what order they will fuck you in, but they move their hands about and talk. I now straddle your face, my tool filling your mouth and you do duty sucking me.

Then the Turks are pushing your thighs higher, and the one inside you brings himself up onto the table, crouching over you, trapping your thighs under his, as he pumps you. The other Turk has moved behind him. He bends over, and I gasp as he reappears standing on his head behind his friend, his legs spread and hanging back, his tool hard and hanging straight down his belly.

The friend reaches back and takes his friend's long tool, feeding the head of it into your hole below his own. You buck at this huge invasion and would have them off you if not trapped under his thighs. I grab your arms and pin those down, knowing this is what you want, but don't want. Two young cocks working inside your single passage so you think you will split apart.

The Turk facing me is going, "Oh, oh," and moving his hips gently as you buck and writhe beneath me. The athletic rear Turk has penetrated you and slowly drives deeper, his cock pointing down and running along the rear of your tunnel, aided by his friend's stroking pull and push.

Soon he is well in and I feel you whimpering. I pull my cock from your mouth and bend to kiss you as they begin to fuck you in an alternating rhythm the way you have fantasized being double fucked. They do it like experienced diggers, alternating their tools in your channel.

I hold your arms back still, stretching your torso out. I lean in to kiss one of the Turks, wanting him to know that I am mesmerized by what he is doing to you. You begin to join the fuck now, meeting the rear Turk's thrusts with yours. I palm your belly, making you moan more and tease your nipples and kiss the Turk again, pleased he had the desire to do this to you.

Both fill you with hot cream and then withdraw, laughing happily as the rear one falls to the ground with a heavy thump.

They laugh and thank you, lying there still with your legs raised, feeling their cum leaking from you as you recover, shocked at what they have done to you, but loving every moment of it. I stand down and move into the space they have vacated between your thighs and add my seed to theirs as you gaze at me, moaning and stroking yourself.

A SURPRISE AT THE LAKE

It was way too hot to be doing anything except cooling down.

I'd spent the day running a class in a room with nothing but fans and then come home to a hot, stuffy, closed-up house. I needed to cool down, and that was why I'd gone down to the lake baths. Swimming in the cool water seemed like an ideal solution.

There was a breeze coming in off the lake, and the sparklingly clean, clear water was refreshingly cool, almost cold. It was heaven after the humid heat of the day, and I did as much floating as swimming, keeping out of the way of a group of teenagers who were the only others there in the water that late.

A couple of small cruisers and a yacht were tied up against the jetty that surrounded the baths. The cafés opposite the water were all good and attracted people from all around the lake so that on a warm summer evening like this the jetties could get quite crowded with boats that had brought people into Toronto for a meal, at the

Mediterranean cafe or The Double Hearts, or one of several others.

After my swim I found a sheltered spot under some Casuarina trees to spread out my towel. It was late, but there was still another hour of daylight and I wanted to have another swim to cool me down again before I went back to my hot house and tried to get a good night's sleep, with nothing but a fan to keep me cool.

I went to sleep lying there. I'd been tired and the cool breeze and soft grass under my towel had combined to make me way too comfortable. When I woke up it was with a start and to find myself lying in the dark. The sky must have been full of clouds, as I couldn't even see any stars when I looked up, and the only light was from the distant road, the jetty running around the baths, the bigger boats tied up there, and what the water reflected back.

I felt pretty stupid to find myself sleeping half the night on the foreshore, but then I heard a grunting noise, quite loud and not too far away. And I knew that must have been what woke me. As I lay there listening, the sounds stopped and started again in the darkness. As I was about to get up and leave, the sounds came again, but it was more of a whimpering sound this time.

I was also sure I heard words mixed in. "Yes," I definitely heard a "yes." I got up as quietly as I could, having a pretty good idea now what was going on and wanting to leave without being noticed.

Of course I had picked up my towel and got my flip-flops back on and was just stepping out from under the trees when the clouds parted and the whole area before me was lit up by a bright silvery full moon. I was still standing in the shadow of the trees and froze where I was, hoping I was out of sight. But in front of me, not ten yards away, the light revealed clearly the source of the noises.

Lying back across the aluminum picnic table was a young man with rippling muscles arching his back and moaning, while standing below him between his raised thighs, with his back three-quarters to me, was another muscular young male whose butt muscles clenched and relaxed as he plowed the ass of the one stretched out before him on the table.

I felt my cock jump inside my shorts at the sight and the sounds, and I stayed frozen. The guy being fucked was obviously enjoying it. He was moaning now, and one hand moved over his body, stopping at his nipples as his other hand played with his own long, hard cock and balls. He was big, I could clearly see that and my cock lurched again in my shorts. And the guy fucking him was long too. He was working his friend's ass with deep long strokes, in and out, with the moon glinting on the slick length of him each time he pulled out, I was mesmerized and my own cock lurched higher.

I couldn't stop watching. Both were built like athletes, and both were obviously enjoying what they were doing, or having done to them. The one on the table, in particular, was not holding back in showing his pleasure in what was pumping so deeply in and out of him. After standing there watching and listening to them for a few minutes, I had to push my own shorts down to let out my hardening cock and give it some attention.

The young man lying back on the table seemed to turn his head in my direction, but I doubted he could see me. He was moaning loudly then, and the man with his back to me gave several sharp, shuddering thrusts, deep into him, before holding steady and letting out a deep grunt. He jerked inside his friend's passage a couple of times, and I almost came from imagining his cum shooting inside his friend before he fell forward over his partner.

I came with a huge shudder, going weak as I shot off jolt after jolt.

"Hey, why don't you join us?" a voice said.

I hardly understood someone was talking to me, I was still so shaky.

"Hey," the voice said again, and the guy on top uncurled and turned to me.

"You like what you see? Then come and join in," he said in a deeper slower voice than the one that had spoken before.

I tugged up my shorts in embarrassment as the guy slipped his softening cock out of his friend's gaping ass—I could see the dark patch of his hole in the moonlight. The guy walked over to me. His friend remained lying back on the table, playing his hands over himself, his legs still spread and bent, showing me everything he had on offer. His cock still long and hard as he stroked it slowly.

"Luke wants you to join in," the man, whose butt I'd been watching pumping, said when he was up close. And he reached out to squeeze my deflating tool through my shorts.

I pulled back. "Umm, I'd better go. I don't do it with guys," I said. But I was still not moving far.

"Never wanted to try it?" he asked.

Now Luke was up and coming over too, with his big cock bobbing up near his belly. He moved in behind me and pressed close.

"I saw you stroking off as you watched. I love a guy getting off watching me being fucked. And you liked it, so you must be curious," Luke said. My cock was paying attention to his body rubbing lightly against my back, his cock sliding up and down my crack and hitting my lower back. In fact I couldn't focus on much else.

The guy in front moved in and kissed me. Feeling another man's lips on mine sent a shiver of horrified shock and instant arousal through me, and his hand was inside my shorts before I realized it.

"Nice," he said, and I couldn't make myself disagree—so the kissing went on as Luke's cock stroked up between my now bare butt cheeks.

Then Luke's hands were at my nipples. His sudden rubbing and pinching of them had me moaning, and I realized that I was sandwiched between the two of them and wondered why I didn't get myself un-sandwiched and home.

I made a half-hearted move to leave.

"Don't you want to know what it's like? With another man?" Luke whispered in my ear, his firm hands now making my hard, tingling nipples hum and the rest of my skin shiver as he stroked them all over me. "You'll enjoy it. I saw the way you got off just watching Vince fucking me. Imagine if you were the one doing the fucking?" he said, speaking in a low, sex-filled voice as I felt his rod sliding up and down and he rocked his hips, dry fucking my crease. Then I jumped as I felt his cock slide between my thighs. "You have a lovely cock, yes. Come on, fuck me," he whispered in my ear, as his hand joined Vince's on my hard cock, one playing my slit and cap with a finger as another hand stroked and rotated on my shaft and Luke's cock slid back and forth, massaging my balls.

"Oh God," I moaned loudly.

Luke's pubes sliding against my butt, his other hand on my thighs, my chest, "Oh Christ," I groaned, throbbing under their attentions as Vince pushed in closer, moving his mouth to my hair and neck, his tongue snaking around on my throat.

"No," I said huskily, "I have to go," and I made another move, but even I knew it was a half-hearted gesture.

Yes, I was curious, especially after the way watching them fuck had made me feel. Especially the way I felt sandwiched between them. I was torn, giving in, just as I heard voices. Suddenly, I was frozen with fear that whoever was coming would see me like that, sandwiched between the two young hunks, and that they would report me to the school and that I would be out of a job. I now had no doubts about my need to leave immediately, and when the voices had moved on, I had every intention of roughly pushing Vince aside and going.

"I'm sorry, I have to go," I hissed, pulling free as soon as it was quiet, dragging my shorts back up, and grabbing my towel.

I didn't look back as I walked hurriedly to my car, trying to look innocent, and relieved that I didn't actually meet anyone. I ached for release, my cock still throbbing. In the car I jerked off to the memory of Vince's cock stroking in and out of Luke's ass.

"Shit." I could still feel Luke's cock slipping under my balls, and I knew I wanted to fuck him.

Then he was standing there, leaning into the car window, turning my head and kissing my mouth as I moaned helplessly. "They're gone, and we've got a boat," he said. "With a big private cabin. So come on, come for a ride onto the lake," he added as his groping hand found my package.

I looked at him, seeing his erection pressing against his shorts.

"Shit," I said.

* * * *

We'd anchored out by Green Point and down in the cabin Vince resumed his kissing and stroking down my throat and chest. But Luke lay back on the bed and, fixing his eyes on mine, raised and spread his legs to show me what he had, as he stroked his cock back to full size. I was soon moaning again and focused on his slitted eyes and cock until he moved a hand beneath his balls to his asshole and slid a finger inside himself. I nearly lost it at the sight.

"Oh, yes," I moaned loudly as Vince sucked at my nipples alternately and probed my slit with his little finger, making me lurch and grunt.

Luke was smiling and working another finger into his hole and pumping himself with small strokes, "I think he's ready, Vince," he said in a husky voice.

Vince turned to look at him and released me. I moved to the end of the bed as Luke's eyes followed me and he whispered, "Fuck me, Chris. Hard, deep. Oh, yes, fuck me with that beautiful cock of yours."

I was convinced already. I stood for a moment, bending and joining two of my fingers to the two he already had inside himself. Me almost coming as he moaned. Then he reached both hands out for my hips as I directed my cap to his entrance. I had expected more resistance, but after a push past his rim, I slipped in smoothly, unable to stop myself driving deep for maximum penetration. He arched and moaned under me as Vince pressed in behind and ran his hands over my butt cheeks.

I had barely started to fuck Luke when I bucked and came, then bucked and shot off again deep inside his passage. I stayed there inside him panting as he ran his hands over my hips and belly, his legs running up my sides and resting on my shoulders. Behind me Vince was kneeling, parting my cheeks and licking my ass. I shuddered as I went with it, and he began to play with my hole, as I stroked Luke off, watching his eyes narrow and his body undulate and twist as he ejaculated up to his face and chest. My tool still resting happily inside him, waiting.

CLIMBING AYERS ROCK— ULURU

Ayers Rock—Uluru—wasn't somehow the way I had imagined it. It was big, sure, but it didn't tower over the landscape surrounding it. It just sat there like something sleeping, curled up in the desert among the Spinifex and the dusky green clumps of grevillea and small shaggy desert oaks. Around its base taller, twisted oak trees grew in its shady nooks and crannies.

The rock was red, the desert was red, the unmade road was red. Everything was red—except the vegetation.

"It changes color," Gerry was saying enthusiastically, "During the day, all the time. Sunrise and sunset are the most spectacular changes; we'll see that this evening. And I've booked us on the bus for the sunrise viewing."

We stood at the base of the rock where the climb began. But at the start of the climb there were far too many plaques put up to commemorate people who had lost their lives trying to reach the top. Jeezus, I thought, looking at them. This was supposed to be a relaxing holiday, not an extreme sports challenge.

"I think I'll give it a miss," I said to Gerry. My feelings were only confirmed by looking up and not being keen on the slope and the thick chain the climbers were pulling themselves up with. It looked like hard work, and it was a very hot day.

"But that's one of the highlights of this trip, David. Climbing the rock. I mean, it's probably the highlight," he said, looking up with that awed gaze he always got at monuments. I could tell. We'd been to a lot of monuments, both natural and man-made.

"Definitely," I said in my positive voice. No way was I killing myself climbing a big red rock whatever it was called.

"You're sure? I mean it's an experience. You'll miss it. This is a once-in-a-lifetime opportunity," he wheedled, though he only looked at me briefly with his big, soulful eyes, his mind already straining upwards, mentally preparing to go.

I'd also miss one chance of dying high up, I thought. "No. You go. You'll get there faster without me anyway," I replied, trying to sound as if I was thinking of him.

Gerry's gaze was already back on the rock. He certainly wasn't going to miss out on reaching the top of Ayers Rock just because I was being unadventurous. I watched him stand for a moment at the base, sizing the climb up. And then he was off, long strides high stepping him up that first steep bit to the chain. A scrawny-looking European couple swept past me and were climbing right behind him, a huge camera bag bouncing on the guy's skinny backside.

Gerry had some kind of weird natural affinity for wiry outdoor European couples. They often appeared at our dinner table, where the three of them would regale each other with the gory details of month-long jungle treks, where the size of both the blisters and local insects seemed to predominate as topics of conversation. I had no doubt

41

that he and the couple climbing behind him would be firm friends by the time he returned to the hotel.

I got back onto the air-conditioned coach and enjoyed a cool, if dull, ride around the base of the rock. I was curious about what may have gone on at the closed-off aboriginal men's sacred sites. Some were initiation sites, including one in the caves at the foot of the huge erect-penis-like slab of split rock clinging tightly to the side of the main body of Uluru—Ayers Rock. Unfortunately, our guide was uncommunicative when I asked for details.

I wondered too how the aboriginals had got the big, white figure drawn in the recess high up at the other end of the rock. But I wasn't really interested enough to press for information when the guide's commentary moved on after saying not much about it.

Back at the hotel it was still early and breakfast time for some of the tourists. I wandered out to the poolside and ordered a coffee and sat under the white sails covering the area, drinking it. Some sundried and overbrowned local was perched on a stool at the nearby poolside bar, regaling anyone who'd listen with stories of his days shooting camels in the desert, and I gazed about idly happy to do nothing for the day.

We'd climbed Kings Canyon the day before and wandered around Alice Springs the day before that, so I knew I didn't need any more exercise. Well, not that kind. The other kind of exercise had been in short supply the last couple of weeks, and I was starting to notice it. Definitely starting to notice it, I realized, my attention suddenly latching onto a rather handsome guy sitting alone at a small table nearby.

Bloody climbing, I thought, for a moment remembering the sight of Gerry's ass determinedly making its way up the path to the chain. And it was a moment before I refocused and found I had been staring at the stranger and that he was smiling right back at me. His smile gave me a nice jag in my arousal department. Then I looked away. It was nice to be noticed, but I was faithful, well I didn't fuck outside marriage, as Gerry put it. He didn't, I didn't. We were both just like that, and we liked barebacking each other, knowing it was safe. Which didn't mean there hadn't been an occasional something, but always short of the real thing.

Then the handsome stranger suddenly got up and came over to my table.

"Hi, I'm Max," he said in a nice American drawl. "So you aren't taking in any sights today?"

Up close he looked even better, and he stroked his shorts up high and smiled.

"No. No. And you?" I asked, obviously staring, quite aware that he was interested and had something pretty sizeable on offer.

The camel shooter was still droning on loudly about camels being feral.

"No, I stayed home today," he smiled. "I'm not really into outdoor exercise, especially in this heat. I'm more of an indoor exercise man. What about you, do you fancy indoor exercise, um . . . I didn't catch your name?"

"David," I offered. "Um, yes. I like both," I said weakly, knowing I felt horny but still not sure how far I wanted to go, feeling Gerry was watching me from somewhere high on the rock.

But I was also annoyed with Gerry. There hadn't been any decent sex since we'd left home two weeks before. Sure he'd tried the night before, but he'd fallen asleep while we were still kissing and playing about, and that had left me even more annoyed with him.

"So, wanna come back to my room for . . . some exercise?" he asked, fixing me with his smile.

He was making me hot. Everything was hot. "I don't know," I said, moving in my chair, my cock filling enough to need relocating to be comfortable. "My partner's

43

climbing the rock, and I'm not sure when he'll be back." If I was going to mess about, I sure didn't want Gerry walking in on us or coming looking for me. I was a bit shocked at how easily I was letting myself be drawn into considering going with Max.

"Oh," he gave me a sharp look. "Well, if he's climbing the rock, he won't be back till after 11:30. Plenty of time," he said. It was just gone 9:00 AM. "My party's due back earlier," he added coolly, looking about the pool at what else was available, giving me the message that if I didn't take up his offer quickly he'd take it elsewhere.

My excitement at the thought of some decent action was making me harder, while my annoyance with Gerry, added to the threat of seeing Max walk away, combined to undermine my resistance.

"Sure." I'd made up my mind. "Why not?" I surprised myself and nearly blocked out the gremlin in my head yelling, "Hey, you're planning on being unfaithful to Gerry." Instead, I thought back "Ten whole years I'm faithful, and once I'm not."

Max's room was bigger than ours, with a wide view to the rock itself. "Great room . . . ," I started to say, but he had his mouth on mine and his pants unzipped and was pulling my hand to his growing cock before I could get the words out.

I had only touched Gerry's and mine for so many years that they had worn grooves in my fist and my fingers flicked and stroked them with the expertise born of years of intimacy. I felt momentarily lost as my hand tried to come to terms with this new piece of meat that didn't fit, and I felt like laughing.

The kiss was quickly over. Then I was vaguely wondering how many hands he had as I felt my own pants fall free and his right hand was massaging my left butt cheek. Part of me wanted things to slow down, but the horny unfucked for a fortnight part was only too happy to cooperate.

"Hmm," he grunted, "head down," he said, pushing my head down. I knelt in front of him and got lost working the long, thick piece he had.

It was standing strongly, slightly curved to his belly, and I started playing my tongue and mouth over his cap while my fingers went to his balls. He pushed his tool down with one hand and grasped the back of my head with the other. He knew what he wanted.

He knew exactly what he wanted, and I was pulled along by his insistence I satisfy his need. He had a firm hold on my head, and I had no choice but to try swallowing him as he pushed his hips forward and forced himself in further.

He was soon moaning, "Oh yes," and groaning, "That's great." I gagged and sucked on what he was feeding me, as he fucked my face.

Then he pulled out and was pulling me up and gave me a brief kiss. "Hey, now the main event," he said with a gleaming white, toothy grin, and I was being propelled back onto the long mirror-backed dresser.

"I like to watch," he said as he stripped off my pants and lubed me up. "You like to watch a nice big cock plowing you, Dave?" he asked as he dropped his own pants and kicked them off.

Dumb question I managed to think as I widened my legs and eased my butt up on the dresser and rolled my hips under. I was leaning back on the bench and the long mirror at an angle, so Max was quarter turned to the mirror, and he had my legs arranged so I could see his fingers pushing at my hairy ass and he could see everything in the mirror too.

He wrapped a hand about my cock, and I was begging, "God, do it. Do it." It was a long time since I had felt so ready. "Yes, yes," I gasped as he worked his fingers into me and spread me, me still gasping he was going so quick. Even his strong, thick fingers were making me open more than I did for Gerry when he fucked me.

He was doing a magic job on my tool too, his thumb working about my head, his fingers applying pressure just right. "Yes, hey, fuck me," I was grunting. And he did.

"Nice tight ass," he said, "real nice." I felt his fingers leaving me and looked and saw his purple cap wearing a condom and pushing at my entrance. I wanted it inside me. I moved my hips to him and widened my thighs, making it easier for him, but still whimpering as he worked in.

"Hey yes," he grunted, and as he penetrated halfway into me, I shot off, sending cream over my belly and thighs. But I continued to moan as I got my breath back and he worked his tool further up into me. I couldn't remember if I had ever had anything so big trying to fit in me before. It sure didn't feel like it. When he finally had it all in, I was gasping with the strain and totally stuffed. It took a few moments for me to adjust to him. Then I still gasped and whimpered when he started to fuck me.

I was moaning and moving my hips to match Max's rhythm when I suddenly saw Gerry's distressed face before me and realized with a stab of regret that I loved him but could never again look him in the eyes and say I'd always been faithful to him. The thought hardly lasted a moment though before I nearly got lost again in the great fucking I was getting. But it was a while before I completely lost myself again. Gerry's distressed look had taken the edge off me, and I knew he was worth a hundred Maxes.

Max not only had technique and a huge tool, he also had stamina. I was moaning loudly and rehardened when he finally came inside me. I got my breath for a moment as he pulled out and stripped off the condom. Now it was my turn, I thought. I took him by the shoulders and wrapped my legs around his hips and pulled him close to me and into a kiss.

Max pulled back, "Hey man, I'm not into kissing much, just sex," he said, and I was a bit disappointed but needed to take my turn with him too much to worry about anything else.

I turned Max and pushed him forward, down along the bench I'd been lying back on before. He put up some resistance, but I held him down, pushing his thighs apart with one of mine and wrapping my other leg around his free one. Then I was running two fingers into his entrance. He'd made it clear we were no more than two males getting our rocks off, and I was back in full heat now and had no problem with it being like that.

Max's resistance let up as I finger fucked him and finally he groaned, "Yes, yes." I knew I had the right technique for him after all, and in a little while I was in and plowing him, first with shallow strokes, then deeper ones, and he was moaning and rocking his hips in time with mine. I showed him I had a bit of stamina too before I finally pulled out and came in the small of his back. He stroked himself off with a grunt.

A few moments after he'd come Max stood up and said, "Thanks man, time to clean up now. Gotta look fresh for the family."

He handed me my clothes, and it was obvious he wanted me dressed and out of there ASAP.

I didn't argue, even though it would only have taken a moment to wash the cum off before I dressed. I returned to my room feeling that I'd missed something. But physically I felt very well satisfied and mellow, so after I showered I lay down and was asleep in moments. I woke to a buzzing noise and it took a few rings before I realized it was the hotel phone.

"Is that David Thorne?" a man's voice asked.

"Yes," I replied sleepily.

"It's Jack Conroy, the manager here, you're sharing your room with Gerry Young, are you?"

"Yes," I answered, something suddenly starting to crawl up my spine. "Yes. Has something happened? He was . . ."

"If you can just come to reception, sir," Jack replied calmly.

"Tell me . . . " I started to say then just threw the phone down and took off.

All sorts of things were going through my head, and the sight of the memorial plaques at the start of the climb up the rock was just one of them.

There'd been an accident, they said, and a car took me to the clinic next to the police station. I was shaking by now and feeling guilty. God, was I feeling guilty. This would never have happened, I kept thinking irrationally, if I hadn't been fucking Max. Gerry was going to die because I'd been horny and fucked with some oversexed Yank.

In a flood of relief that Gerry was alive, I was allowed in to see him. He looked deathly pale lying on the examination table. And bruised and cut. He looked over at me, and suddenly we were both crying and I had hold of his hands and he was mumbling incoherently.

"It's OK," I said firmly. "It's OK, you'll be fine," I talked reassuringly, having no idea what had happened, just incredibly relieved he was alive and conscious.

"I slipped. I was taking a photo for them, at the top, and I stepped back . . . and . . . and I slipped. I thought I was going to die, Dave. I did. I just felt empty. Then I saw you, and my hand caught in a crack in the rock," he managed to get out between gasps and sobs.

Then he held up his damaged hand, and I wished he hadn't, even roughly bandaged, it was obvious it was a mess. And I could see the camera bag bouncing on the wiry European's backside at the start of the climb and could picture exactly what had happened—and wouldn't have, if I had been there.

48

Then the ambulance was ready to take him to the plane to Alice Springs, and I was ushered out of the examination room while they got him ready. The wiry European couple were huddled together in the waiting room and looked up as I entered.

"He stepped back . . . and just slid off the rock— taking our photos," the husband stammered. "It's very smooth and curved, he just disappeared over the edge. But we got a rope and I . . ."

He talked on but I wasn't listening any more. Inside I knew just when Gerry had stopped falling.

CONFUSION TIME

"Shit," I exclaimed. I had been in the middle of writing an e-mail when the power went out.

"Shit," I said again, as I fell over the archive box I had forgotten was sitting in the middle of my study floor. I finally made it to the window and looked outside to see that every other house in the street still had its lights on, so the power outage was restricted to my house. Fortunately, I knew where the flashlight was, because I had replaced the battery only a few days before. Once I was armed with it, I headed downstairs.

The ground floor of my house was in the process of being converted into a large self-contained apartment. During the day a steady stream of tradesmen came and went from there, at great expense to me and to the increasing concern of my personal banking manager. But it was almost finished now and was looking quite impressive, even without the final decorating done.

I couldn't understand what might have happened for me to lose the power. Everything about the wiring was new and there had been no problems. The rear doors were still loose, though, and I wondered vaguely if someone might have broken in. I moved the flashlight in a wide arc to cover the whole of the small area at the bottom of the stairs before I stepped down. I strained my ears and thought I heard something beyond the door, but when I froze and listened, I heard nothing and felt foolish.

The fuse box had been relocated during the renovation and was now in an inset cupboard in the shared entryway, grandly called the "foyer" on the plans, which opened onto the street. I opened the door to the foyer and quickly shone the flashlight around the cluttered space before I stepped out, wondering why there was so much building material stacked up in there. I shone my light onto the power box and saw it was open. The workmen never seemed to tidy anything up, and it annoyed me at times, because I had to climb thorough their mess to leave the house or get back inside. I stepped over to the box and looked inside. The main power switch was off, which was odd. I flicked the switch back across, and the outside light, visible through the fanlight over the front door flickered on. I stood there for a moment, puzzled; as there was no way that the power switch could have gone off unless someone had turned it off. A sudden chill ran through me as I heard a sound behind me and I swung around.

The next thing I can clearly remember was half waking, with a terrible headache. I moved and it exploded in my head and I had to freeze still until it eased. The bright light was hurting my eyes, which seemed wrong somehow. Then I vaguely wondered what had happened and imagined I must be lying on the floor of the foyer I had been walking into.

"Are you OK?" someone asked, and I got another stab of pain as I turned too quickly to find the owner of the voice.

"Ahhh," I gasped, and a reassuring hand was on my shoulder.

"Just relax. You had a bad knock," Roger said, pushing me gently but firmly back.

I wondered vaguely what my architect was doing there at night. But I was also relieved that someone had found me, as I was not feeling too good. "What happened?" I asked him.

"I don't know, I Just came back to check on the progress, and when I turned the light on, I saw you lying here, out cold. I'd better get you an ambulance," he added.

"No," I gasped, making a grab for his arm, with my head clearing quickly now I was awake. "No. I feel OK. Just a bit dizzy."

Roger settled back down beside me and I tried to sit up again, but I was overcome by dizziness once more, and he had to help me. He had an arm about my back and under my arm and was holding me quite firmly. And suddenly I found his neck in front of my face and his mouth not too far away. I leaned in to him, and he turned a fraction, so that almost accidentally our lips met. I hesitated and so did he, so that we stayed that way for a moment before I made the move to make it a proper kiss. Then there was no hesitation on his part.

"Hey," he said, when we pulled apart. "Nice. You can't be feeling too bad then, so no ambulance. But I'd better get you upstairs."

I let him help me up, not leaning on him much more than I really needed to. And I wasn't too far out of it to appreciate the concern in his deep, velvety voice.

"Thanks," I said, unable to say more just then. I was still shaky and could not have made my way back upstairs without Roger's help.

When we reached the top of the stairs, he said, "I think you should go to bed, and then I'll get you something to drink."

"Sorry to put you to so much trouble," I replied. "But I don't think I could have got upstairs without your help."

"No trouble," he replied, helping me to my bedroom, me very aware of his mouth close by my ear.

I turned to him impulsively and fed my arms around his neck, and we fell into another deep kiss. I had always fancied Roger, but he had made it clear he already had a partner and that it was a monogamous relationship. I was waiting for him to say something now. But instead he moved his arms about my waist, pulling me into him and eagerly delving into my mouth with his tongue.

His partner, Hiram, was older than he was and was a wealthy property developer of the better kind. He was famous for his large inner-city renovation and conversion projects. Turning big old impractical but beautiful homes and old office buildings into luxury apartments and townhouses was his specialty, and Roger had found his place as the firm's principal architect. He still did private work, though, which was how I had come to engage him. He was good, and I wanted my small project to have the right sort of style to it. But it was also well known that Hiram was the jealous kind. It was common knowledge a previous lover of his had been dumped and badly hurt when he had been caught seeing another man.

When we disengaged from our kiss, I could feel Roger pressing his hard rod against mine. "Better get you to bed," he said huskily.

He moved me backwards as we took little frantic bites at each other's lips, and I ran my hand to his zipper and opened it so I could get to what he had inside there. He was larger than I expected, and still growing. We made it to the bedroom, and he pushed me back onto the bed and knelt over me, straddling my thighs as he pulled off my shirt.

As he dropped his mouth to my right nipple and lipped and sucked it, I realized that my dizziness had gone about the time of our second kiss. Then I curved my chest up to him as he began teasing the hard lump between his teeth. Soon he had my mouth again while unzipping me and roughly pushing my pants and briefs down under my balls and grasping my engorged cock.

"Nice," he whispered again, as he moved his mouth to my left nipple and bit that, sending a shiver of anticipation through me, back to my rim, making it twitch. He was resting on one hand and only had the other to use on me. "Stroke yourself," he whispered, then released me and worked his hand under my ass and fed his fingers between my cheeks as his thighs kept mine pressed to the bed. His hand was strong and large, and he grasped my cheek and pulled his fingers down the crease to my rim and fed one finger into me before I realized it. "Nice and tight," he said huskily, removing his hand and moving his hips up me so that his cock joined mine and he could take both and stroke them together.

I was desperate to have him inside me and wanted to open my legs and invite him in, but he had me trapped tight. I worked his shirt off with my free hand and began to feel his hard abs and his muscular chest. He was harder and leaner than I'd expected; stronger too. I pinched and rolled his nipples, making him gasp. "I want you to fuck me," I said brokenly, getting close to coming already.

"Good," he grunted, "because I'm going to," he added in a deep, low growl.

Hearing him say it like that was enough to have me shoot off all over his belly and my chest. "Good," he said, releasing me and sliding off the bed, pulling my pants and shoes off me as he went.

I lifted my legs and opened them ready for him, but he laughed. "No, I want you over the end railing."

I looked down, confused, knowing the railing was quite high. I slept in a fancy low-timber bed with polished rails across the head and foot, five at the foot, seven at the head. I slid to the floor and Roger led me down to the foot of the bed and had me climb onto the second rail. Then he spread my feet wide apart until my hips were level with the top rail and I could just fold forward over it. My cock was pushed back painfully between my legs, but my asshole, I realized, was at a very good height for him to work with his tongue and fingers. He commenced to loosen me up, pulling my cock back in one hand and working my ass with his other hand and his mouth.

I was soon rehardening, as his probing fingers went deep, making me moan with pleasure as well as leaving me well opened for him when he released my cock. My head was resting on the bed, looking back at him, and he reached through and pulled my face close to the rail. Then he fed his cock through the gap and into my mouth. I was tied up in knots but reached through the rails to take his hips and pull him to me because I wanted everything he was doing to my ass and more.

Then he licked me between my balls and hole before his tongue rimmed me again and he was feeding his fingers back into me, rotating them as he fucked my face in hard strokes that had me gagging at each inward landing, even though he couldn't get his full length into me through the rails. Then he had both hands at my ass, and I jerked and grunted as he pulled at my entrance, painfully widening and spreading me with the fingers of both hands as his hard tongue was searching inside me.

He was stroking my spot inside with his long fingers, and I was having trouble keeping up my sucking. I was desperate to come and to be filled, and starting to feel stretched and sore in my spread legs as well as my ass.

"Now," he said, "stand up and lean back to me." He had his hands on my back as I stood up with relief, my legs cramped and strained. Then he made me lean back and take my legs up over the top rail so I was hanging from it, leaning back against him as he lowered my ass to his cock. I reached back around his neck to support myself and arched my back, moving myself into a perfect position as he took one hand and fed his cock into my well-stretched and opened hole, while I descended on it. I gasped at his entry, because he was thick as well as long, and with my legs already strained I was going down on him uncontrollably quickly.

I cried out as he entered me to the hilt, and I landed against his crotch, feeling his pubic hair slippery under my stretched ass. He pushed me forward, and I grabbed the top rail and lifted myself up before he lightly pushed my hips down and I descended on him again. He stood there leaning back to get full depth. He worked me like that, an uncomfortable fucking machine as he powered deep into me. I didn't want to stop as I worked myself faster and harder on him, but he slowed me and started bringing his hips up hard to meet my descent. I jerked and moaned at each shared thrust. Then he had a hand roughly stroking my own cock, caught between my belly and the bed rail and I felt him lurch as he came inside me, coming myself from the feel of it. Then he bounced me on his cock again and once more shot off deep inside me.

When he was done, he pushed me forward and I pulled myself up over the railing and collapsed forward onto the bed, achingly well fucked and filled, but wanting more.

Roger crawled up beside me and spooned me against him, then took my chin and brought my face about into a deep kiss while he stroked my chest and belly with his other hand. He refilled quickly and fed his cock into my passage, still well opened and lubricated with his cum. I sighed and moaned as he plowed me for a long time with deep long strokes until we both came, me loving the feel of his hot cum shooting deep inside me. He stayed buried as I lay back, spooned against him and exhausted.

The next thing I remember was half waking with a terrible headache. I moved and it exploded in my head and I had to freeze still, until it eased. Then I vaguely wondered what had happened, because I no longer felt my bed under me, and for a moment I imagined I was again lying on the floor of the foyer where Roger had found me

"Are you OK?" someone asked, and I got a small stab of pain as I turned too quickly to find the owner of the voice.

"Ahhh," I moaned and a hand was on my shoulder, as I blinked in the bright light.

"Just relax, you had a bad knock," Roger said, feeling my head over and finding the sore patch that had become a lump, then pushing me gently but firmly back.

I reached for him, clasping his neck with my arms as my head spun, but he pushed my hands away. "You'll be OK," he reassured me, and I looked about, suddenly confused but already less dizzy. I realized I was dressed as I had been when I'd first come down to check the power box, and I saw sunlight streaming through the open street door.

"What are you doing here Roger?" I asked.

"I came by to check on progress," Roger replied, "and found you lying here."

I sat up, feeling much better already. "But weren't you here before?" I asked him.

"I just got here," he replied "Are you going to be okay?"

I was trying to think but was unable to, wondering if I had dreamed it all. My legs, hips and arms ached, but that was not surprising if I had spent the night on the bare timber floor of the foyer and only dreamed the wild fucking Roger had given me upstairs on my bed.

Roger didn't go far away but was obviously looking over the work of the last few days. "It's looking good," he said, returning to me. "Coming on very well."

I was right to stand up by myself by then, and my head had cleared, "Were you . . . ?"

"Are you ready, Roger?" a voice called from the entrance. I recognized it as Hiram's. "Hello Jim," he said, seeing me, "I'm double parked out here," he added fretfully for Roger's benefit.

"Are you OK?" Roger asked me, and I nodded, knowing I could make it upstairs alone now. "Then I'll catch you later," he said, smiling, and left.

DELAYED APPOINTMENT

I had not really been aware of the noise of the big engines until there was a loud jarring grinding and the engine noise stopped. The ferry began to roll with the swell, and the murmur of voices rose in the background.

"What's happening?" I asked the man in the tiny snack bar set in under the main staircase to the upper deck.

"Engines stop" and a shrug was the reply. "Is an old ferry, but a good one. But sometimes the ferries, they stop."

"Oh, what happens now? I've got an appointment in Manly at 11.30," I said, not actually thinking the snack bar man could do much to help me.

"Another ferry come," he said. "They put you all on that, but you will be late. You call them, let them know." He said that while making a phone-to-ear play with his hand, assuming I had my mobile phone on me, like 80 percent of the other ferry passengers did, including 99.9 percent of those under forty. I was the .1 percent who didn't. I hadn't wanted to be reachable today, so my mobile phone was sitting at home. I was stuck with being late. When the replacement ferry arrived to get us off, it went straight to Manly. I was two hours late, but I was there and things looked good, so I might as well see about doing what I had come to do.

The receptionist looked up at me with a warm, expectant "you look good enough to eat" smile when I entered the foyer.

"Mike. Mike Sands," I said.

"Good afternoon, I'm sorry, we were expecting you earlier . . ."

"Yes, sorry. The ferry broke down, and I couldn't call to let you know. Harvey . . ."

The receptionist's expression had passed from warm welcome to fear to uncertainty at what to do with me, to "I must keep smiling."

She discovered an answer and tried to re-ignite the warmth of her welcoming smile.

"I'm sorry, Mike. Harvey has gone to a meeting. He waited . . ."

I was sure that meant he had gone off to a long lunch. I knew just enough about Harvey to know that. He probably had waited a while for me to arrive, though. Maybe fifteen minutes. But I was always going to be later than that.

"He won't be back till late this afternoon. I'm afraid none of the other senior—"

"Are you waiting for someone?" a voice asked behind me after I heard the entrance door close with a discrete swish and dull thunk.

The receptionist looked relieved, and I turned to the speaker. He was tall and good looking, sporting a short, clipped silver beard with a full head of steel-gray hair, set on a handsome head that topped a well-looked-after body that moved gracefully and like that of a man some years younger. It was hard to know how old the new arrival was. Anywhere from late forties to sixty. I automatically smiled at such an agreeable sight, and my eyes made an appraising trip down to his tan loafers and then back up to his face and his dark twinkling eyes. His perfect teeth flashed at me when he smiled back, and he was more than sufficiently inviting for me to follow him into a very nice office. And of course I had business to do with the firm of Scorso, Field, and Manwell.

"Take a seat, Mike. I'm Tony Scorso, the senior partner," he said with that wide, engaging smile. Very kissable lips, I decided. Yes, I had no trouble being interested in him and showing it.

Now that we were in his private office he was being a bit more open in his inspection of me than he had been in the reception area, though still pretending he wasn't interested, and maybe he wasn't. Maybe he was just assessing my net worth and whether I was worth taking time to talk to. But I had felt his eyes on my crotch when he had a chance of a good view, and I knew the jeans I had on were quite good at suggesting I had even more down there then I probably did. Not that I didn't have plenty to offer.

Tony played on his keyboard and glanced at the computer screen. "You wanted to discuss a commercial development proposal with Harvey?"

They obviously kept good records.

"And how is Charlie Tinsdell?"

Very good records. I had needed a reference and had said I'd been referred to them by Charlie, though that wasn't strictly true.

"Charlie is in the Bahamas, enjoying some company and some sun." Charlie had also taken a young blonde model who had made the cover of *Cleo* off to the island to show everyone that he was still getting some of what his wife was no longer giving him. But he had the good manners to go a long way away from their friends to do it. Little did they know what Charlie really liked to get.

"He has a house there, I believe," Tony replied politely.

"Yes. A very nice pseudo tropical palace," I said with a chuckle, "He was very complimentary of what you could do, and might do for me," I added, my eyes glued to his and my voice dropping down to what I was told was a mesmerizing hum so it sounded like I was saying something else. Tony cleared his throat and tried to sit up straighter.

"Look, do you have time to discuss this now?" I asked, relaxing back in my seat. "Because if you do, I was stuck on that ferry for two hours and could do with a coffee and maybe a bite to eat."

"Of course. I was on the same ferry, and I missed lunch too. The ferry shop doesn't exactly offer much that's healthy or appealing. Let's go to the café opposite. They do great coffee and good food. My shout," Tony replied cheerfully. I knew he'd been on the ferry. I had noticed him.

As we left his office and he held the door open for me, I went so close to him we touched almost all the way up our sides, and I also lay a hand gently and briefly in the small of his back as I passed. He reacted just how I was sure he would when I decided to do that. He was getting me hot and bothered, I admit. He had sex appeal, and I hoped I was doing the same to him. Very much hoped.

I like good-looking mature men who can't keep their eyes off me. Is that a surprise? And I was horny—but then I usually am. Horny is my middle name. Martin Horny Sanderson, oops, I mean Mark, oh, and Sands. Mark Horny Sands.

At the café I made sure we wound up at a small table in a dark corner inside, instead of outside, with everyone else sitting on the sunlit footpath with a view of the pines and surf at Manly beach.

"Good food?" I asked, picking up the menu.

"Definitely," Tony replied. "And good coffee. Great coffee." He seemed a bit nervous. I like to have that effect on a man, and I smiled approvingly back, my eyes lingering on his till his dropped and he seemed to blush. I love a man who can blush. It always sends a shiver up my spine and a surge of blood to where it matters when a man blushes for me. I love even more a man who can look as if he wants it all while he blushes. And Tony was almost doing that. He just needed to know what "all" of it was with me. I wanted Tony even more.

I was close to him at the small table I had picked out, and I knew he could smell me, as I could him. He smelled fresh, almost a tang of sea air on him, from the ferry trip, I suppose. And he wore a light cologne, something nice and woody. I have been told my body smells very sexy, like warm honey, and I don't hide it, so I hoped Tony enjoyed the close-up smell also. He seemed to, as his pants were looking just a bit occupied in his lap, but I had to sort of lean over a bit to see it, so I only got a glimpse. I didn't want to be too obvious. After all we were here to discuss business, and I had important business to do with Tony.

"I suppose I should be telling you about the project I have in mind," I said, as soon as we had ordered from a perky young blonde waitress, who sounded Swedish. Manly is full of young foreign backpackers. Plenty of eye candy on the sand and in the nearby streets in summer when the weather suits lying on the beach in a Speedo, or a bikini, if that's your thing. "I want something that opens onto the water," I said. "And an open fire. One of those 1950s sort of Wright-style natural stone fireplaces that takes up half a wall, with the rest mostly glass."

"You have the site already?"

"Oh, yes. On the Lake at Torno Bay, and we have approval to remove the old shack there and build a triplex on the site. The main house will be for me and the other two will be for sale. Similar, but smaller, and with only limited water views, though there is some slope on the site so the rear unit should have clear views from the upper level."

I produced a folded piece of paper from the bag I had with me and unfolded it on the table between us. There was barely room for the plan, and Tony's head was almost touching my chest when he bent over to peer at it in the dim light.

"Um, can we move to a larger table perhaps?" he soon suggested, looking about at the other empty tables, and then at me, smiling a sexy and disarming smile. "I would really like to be able to have a good look at this."

I knew he only wanted big multimillion-dollar projects nowadays, but he wasn't walking away from this yet, and I admired his genuine dedication to his craft.

"Oh sure," I said, and we got up and shuffled over to a larger table with a bench seat on one side. I moved in beside Tony. It was an even better arrangement than the small table I had originally picked. I didn't crowd him though to start with. I let him bend over the site plan and ask questions, and if my fingers brushed his as I pointed out the contours and where I wanted things, well it was a small plan. I also had photos of the views, and he examined them with a sense of excitement, as he should have, because it was a beautiful site. Gently sloping to the water with views to Pulbah Island and facing north. It was a rare find.

Our meals and coffees arrived, and I moved far enough away from him that we could both eat without touching. Except at the knees. Mine occasionally brushed his, and he seemed to not notice it, which made me smile. We talked property and about his projects.

"And the budget for this?" he asked, as he pushed his empty plate away, looking at me appraisingly, now the total businessman even if he didn't seem to have noticed my thigh now pressing against his. He wasn't moving anyway, and I could feel the heat coming off him and had noticed him use a hand to adjust what was obviously taking up a bit more room in his lap than previously.

"We expect it to come in under three million for the three units with landscaping. There will be a horizon lap pool along the lake side of my house, of course, and small spa pools for the other two units and a shared boathouse and larger jetty. I have an old timber forty footer I keep moored at the Spit now, which I will sail there."

"It's not a big project, but it's an interesting one," he replied, looking a bit dreamy and slightly uncertain. "We only do larger developments nowadays, but then there are not many projects like this around. Interesting, small, very high-quality ones." He looked torn.

"I'd really like you to take it on, Tony," I said, laying my hand on his. He seemed to lurch and gulp.

I left my hand there. Where our thighs touched was burning a hole in my flesh. I was getting uncomfortable myself. Basically, I just wanted to drag this man away and into bed and fuck his brains out. "I think I can convince you to take it on," I murmured in my best seduction voice, gently rubbing my fingers over the back of his hand till it shook.

He looked confused and turned away. He pulled his hand away and broke thigh contact and gave an embarrassed laughed. Then he turned back to me, tipping his head to one side as he looked at me.

"Are you coming on to me," he said as if he was making a joke. "I mean—"

"I'm going to make love to you," I replied, speaking slowly and sliding along the bench the few inches that separated us so that my thigh was again pressed to his along its full length, hip to knee. "I like making love to beautiful older men."

He gave a nervous laugh, "Who said I like men?"

"No one," I replied with a shrug and slid an arm along the back of the bench seat behind his back and rested my hand on his shoulder. "But when a big strong young man like me takes you forcefully and hard, I know you will like it. Like it very much," I said, looking him in the eye.

Tony gasped, took tiny breaths, and quivered. I wanted to kiss him forcefully and hated that I couldn't in the café. His lips were trembling, and his eyes were wide as he sat there, mesmerized.

I ran my free hand up his thigh and brushed my fingers across the tent in his pants, then up, pressing against his belly just under the table top, so no one else in the café could see. Then my hand moved down again, and when I found that tent in his pants, I followed it to the base between his parted thighs, which opened wider for me, and then ran my fingers up it again.

"I will ride you to the sound of the waves pounding and crashing on the hot sand," I murmured in his ear as I squeezed his shoulder while the hand lying on his cock squeezed that gently.

He moaned and swallowed hard, then murmured, "No. No, I . . . ," but my eyes held his and he was unable to pull away. I knew he wanted whatever I wanted.

"Come," I said pulling him out from behind the table and out of the café. I knew we'd find a bedroom at the Regent just half a block away. I left the plans there, spread on the table, and even Tony didn't say anything. His eyes were wide and his lips parted and his legs carried him along next to me, my hand in the small of his back guiding him out onto the sunlit street and turning him toward the Regent Tower hotel apartment complex opposite the beach.

We walked in total silence for a few yards, toward the hotel that was only another thirty yards along the road. "I . . .," he stammered. "I have a place here, we can go there," he said, and I put an arm about his shoulders and squeezed.

Tony moved faster then, and I sped up to keep with him. Knowing he'd be doing it on home ground obviously set his mind at ease, and in a few minutes we were in the elevator and I embraced him and pushed him hard against the elevator wall. I ran my hands up and down his body and covered his lips with mine and entered his mouth with my tongue. My right hand quickly unzipped him and reached in to feel the hard rod he had straining to get out from inside there. "So nice," I murmured as I tucked his cock back into his pants and my lips left his while the elevator slowed after the fifteen-floor ride up.

Tony lurched and his lips parted as his eyes hooded and his breath became shallow and rapid.

I stood back from him, leaving him supported by the wall as the elevator stopped, and when the doors slid open, I propelled him out and along the carpeted corridor. Tony got a key out of his pocket with a shaky hand as we hurried along.

At the door of this apartment, I leaned against his back so he could feel what I had ready for him as he struggled to get the key in the lock and open the door. "No. No . . . ," he moaned, "Not here, not . . .," as I rubbed myself up and down his butt, and he was having a lot of trouble getting his key in the door his hands were shaking so much. Finally, I gripped it and guided it to the keyhole for him. We almost fell into the room, and he was jelly as I pushed him against the wall beside the door and grasped his wrists and forced his arms up hard back against the wall as my lips went to his then moved to his throat before returning to his mouth with a bruising kiss.

Lower down I was pressed hard against him, my hips moving fractionally, but enough to rub my dick against his. Two hard rods competing for space. I possessed his mouth, and he struggled fitfully as I pushed harder against him. Then suddenly I pulled back and unzipped his pants and pulled them and his briefs down roughly to the sound of his gasps and oh's.

I swallowed his cock. I am not a great sucker unless in the mood, and he had me almost in that mood as I made love to his already-hard cock. He wanted me. I wanted him. Perfect. But I doubt he knew I wanted to take him hard and heavy and he couldn't get away.

I stood up and we kissed again, but his arms were now wrapping about me and he was pushing his hips at me, wanting more of everything.

I bent over and flipped him over my shoulder, I was bigger and stronger and managed to get away with doing it, his dick pressed to my chest in front. His fists clawed at my back uselessly as he gasped and the surprise overcame him. He was a real man, though, and the short walk to the bedroom with him over my shoulder was not quite as easy as I made out. I was glad when I leaned over and he fell off me onto the tropical pattern of the doona cover on top of the bed. He looked stunned, as he lay there naked apart from his short-sleeved business shirt. He also looked taken and incredibly fuckable. I climbed up and placed my knees on each side of his hips and, grasping his wrists, forced his arms up and out as my mouth found his in another possessive bruising kiss. He suddenly struggled to free his arms, but only weakly so, and I clamped my knees tighter and rested my butt on his thighs.

"I think I need to restrain you," I said to him and pulled my belt free. His wrists were not hard to capture and bind together and attach to the headboard.

Tony's cock was standing up rock hard when I was done.

I happened to glance at the picture on top of his bedside chest as I opened the drawers looking for condoms or lube. "I think I'd better turn her away," I said to him with a smile, turning the picture of Rosemary to the wall. "Oh, no . . . ," he moaned.

I found what I was looking for and counted condoms out and placed them in a row by his head. "One for me, one for me, one for me, one for me, and one more for me, then we will run out and I may have to bareback you," I said with a smile.

"No, no, there are more . . ." he gasped.

"Shhh, be good for daddy," I said.

I stood up on the bed, my feet each side of his hips, looming over him as I stripped off my shirt and unzipped my pants then pushed them and my briefs down, letting him see what he was getting, and he moaned. After kicking my pants off, I dropped to my knees again, encasing his hips and holding our cocks together briefly, mine clearly longer and thicker than his. I got off the bed then and removed my shoes and socks and also his. Then I ripped off his shirt as he gasped and looked afraid.

Finally, I fucked him. Lifting his legs and raising his hips on my thighs and fingering him till he felt ready for me to start feeding my throbbing cock into him. He moaned and writhed and cried out, "Oh no, I can't . . . you are . . . .Oh, oh . . ." But he did take it all, and soon he was moving his hips with mine, and I bent over and kissed him, the perspiration giving his face a sexy damp sheen as he came up my belly That was enough to make me come too. "Condom one, down," I said as I pulled out and removed it. We kissed for a while as I fondled his nipples and belly. Then I kissed his neck and chest and then his nipples, lapping at them before putting on the next condom and turning him over and plunging straight in so that he almost leapt off the bed.

* * * *

The phone was ringing when I let myself into my apartment, but I didn't hurry to pick it up. I knew who it was likely to be.

"Hi," I said when I did answer it at last.

"Where the hell have you been?" the voice on the other end demanded. "I've been calling all night. Why the hell don't you take your mobile with you, and what were you up to anyway?"

"Hello, Charlie, and how are you too?" I replied, amused.

"Humph. It's hot and she's already making those noises. Ha. I have changed my booking and I come back tomorrow instead. And I want to see you."

"Oh, why the rush?" I asked to annoy him.

"You know damn well why. The woman already thinks because I bring her to the Bahamas with me for a week that if she pouts enough, I'm going to leave Muriel for her or take her on as some sort of mistress."

"It's that magnetic effect you have on women, Charlie."

"The money you mean. So where were you? You're changing the subject."

"I was doing a little job for you, Charlie. That one regarding your daughter, Rosemary."

"So is the guy a poof?"

"Does he like making love with men, do you mean?"

"Whatever, you know damn well what I mean, Martin."

"I really want him to do Torno Bay for me, Charlie."

There was a moment's silence. "So you want him to work for you. But we always work together. So what are you saying?"

"I am saying that I think Rosemary should look elsewhere for husband number three and leave Tony to me. I will appreciate him far more than she ever will. And I will get the house I want."

"Martin. I am back in a couple of days; we talk about this," he replied, sounding worried.

"Don't worry, Charlie, there will still be room for you, if that is what you want."

I looked about the apartment I owned. I'd not been poor ever, but seducing my father's old business partner, Charlie, when he had a project I wanted to be included in had worked well for both of us. He had been a very handsome older man fifteen years ago, and I already had a taste for overpowering older men. But Charlie was never going to leave Muriel, and now I wanted a man of my own to come home to.

"There will always be a place for you, Charlie, but I think it's time I had someone at home too, like you have Muriel. And that is about as negotiable for me now as Muriel ever was for you."

There was a long silence as Charlie digested this. "So, what do I tell Rosemary?"

"I don't think you will need to tell her anything, Charlie. I'm sure Tony won't be available to see her any more once she gets back from Italy. And he will be moving soon, of course. You can play the sympathetic father to her."

FINDING HEAVEN

I will always remember the barn. How could I ever forget it? It was a big, corrugated iron one, dull with age and with no windows on the lower level and just one at each end, up in the gable. Tall narrow windows that let light into the loft, while below the barn was dark and silent, cluttered and filled with dust. But I didn't know that when I first saw it.

I came upon it slowly as I emerged onto the top of the mountain, after a steep climb from the bay below, which had taken me through the untouched forest of the national park. And I came at it from the rear, seeing the high window lit with the full afternoon sun, and I saw him there caught in the sun, naked and golden, like some lost angel. Perched up there on the windowsill with his arms spread wide hanging on to the frame. He is the reason I remember the barn so well.

I stopped there, breathing hard, recovering from the climb, and staring, fascinated by the erotic image before me. I was half expecting him to disappear, to be some trick of my mind. I wasn't as young or as fit as I once was, and a dizzy spell had caught me out the day before and left me unsteady for a while.

But no, the golden angel didn't vanish; instead, I now saw that he was looking toward me, and I waved at him. I waited, but he never waved back; he just stood poised on his perch, ignoring me and apparently unconcerned that I was staring at his nakedness. Yes. I was staring at him, drinking him in, and letting his beauty soak into me and send a warm rush though my body. And as my breathing returned to normal, I became increasingly aroused.

Then suddenly I realized that he was falling. His arms were still spread out and he appeared to be standing, but as I watched he slowly began to fall forward. And he didn't make any sound, or any gesture to save himself.

I was frozen and part of me was saying, "It isn't real, this isn't happening," and part of me was screaming "Noooooooooooo." A long, drawn-out cry of rage rising up in me at what he had done as I watched. At what he was doing to himself, and to me.

He continued to fall silently, performing a perfect swan dive, as I stood there frozen, my mouth opening in a silent helplessness, but part of me still saying, "No, it can't be real." It seemed like forever that he fell, but it must have been only moments before he silently disappeared. Then there was a puff of dust and the spell was broken.

I dropped my heavy pack and ran toward the rear of the barn where he had fallen, thinking, "Have I got my mobile? Who will I ring? How do you treat a broken neck? Shit, it's twenty years since I did first aid, shit, shit. Why? Why would he do it? Why to me?"

The grass had only been ankle high where I had been hiking past, but as I ran closer to where he had fallen, it got longer, and thicker. I was imagining broken bones poking out of skin and almost vomited just thinking of it. Then I got within a dozen feet of where I imagined he was and found myself slowed down and almost wading through thick thigh-high grass.

Then I was trying to climb a huge pile of decaying grass clippings and rubbish when I heard a soft moaning, and I finally saw him. He was pulling himself out of the center of the invisible pile of lawn clippings and moaning.

"Fuck it. I can't do anything right," he suddenly shouted and started swearing. "Fuck, fuck. Whyyyyy?"

I was only feet away from him now, but he still didn't seem to know I was there.

"Ouch," he yelped, collapsing in a heap, half buried in dry grass and twigs as I noticed small branches sticking out of the pile he had landed in.

I stopped, only about four feet from him, standing knee deep in vegetation and in danger of twisting something. I was panting again, and he seemed to be crying as he nursed his left arm.

I struggled the rest of the way to him, "Are you OK?" I asked as I reached out to touch him, still afraid I'd find something awful.

He jerked around. "Oh shit," he gaped at me, "Who . . .? Were you . . .? God, did you see? Oh," He seemed completely flustered now. "I'm sorry. I've made a complete mess of it," he wailed, kicking a leg out at the rubbish he was half buried in.

"I should have checked, shouldn't I?" he continued looking up at me, with tears streaking his cheeks. "Garth always told me I was no good at the details. 'You're bloody useless at the detail, Ty,' He was always saying. And I can't even manage to kill myself."

He was young, but not as young as he had looked poised up there in the barn window, and I was in shock myself and started yelling at him, "You frightened the bloody life out of me. Seeing you fall like that. And I am damn glad you didn't get badly hurt. Stop wallowing in self-pity. I hate blood. And I have no idea who to call if you were seriously hurt. I don't even know what the mobile reception is like here."

I sat down beside him, still panting, and he looked at me, peering at me with his mouth open. "See. Details, you think of them," he said with admiration. "I did take my contacts out, though," he added with a flicker of a smile.

For a moment I thought, "The twit can't see. Geez." But then I was looking into his eyes, and god, those blue eyes of his, and I thought instead, "God, how I'd love to be gazing into them as I fuck him."

"You're hurt," I said, pulling myself back to the present situation where I was playing the Good Samaritan. "How's your arm?" I asked, wondering how bad the arm he was nursing was and trying to remember what to do for someone in shock, as he obviously was.

I was worried that some awful injury he couldn't feel yet was being hidden by the rubbish that half covered him. I could see scratches everywhere, small ones that were oozing a drop or two of blood, and a couple of nastier gouges from small twigs that were starting to bleed trickles of blood.

"Come on. You need to get up and, well, get out of here. Do you think . . . um do you think your arm . . . is, um, broken?" I asked him, but not really wanting to know, because I couldn't remember what I was supposed to do if it was.

"Um," he looked down at it sitting against his chest. "Um, it hurts, but I am not sure. I think I landed on it. It may just be bruised."

"What a stupid thing to do," I couldn't stop myself saying. "You could have given me a bloody heart attack."

But that wasn't the real problem just then. He had turned more toward me, and I now had his half hard cock just in front of me. Christ, I was already dying to fuck him and now he was showing me his goods. His skin was pale all over, a healthy glowing pale, not the dull pale skin of a shut-up city person. And there was nothing tidied up about him; his golden hair spread out from his bush, up his belly, and was also sprinkled thickly over his balls and inside his thighs. His cock was a hairless, pale, veined sausage with its red head just poking out of his foreskin.

I couldn't help myself. I was in shock. I was running on the primitive drive to mate that overcomes us all when we have just escaped death or seen another do it. I slid my hand under his tool and lifted the head to my open mouth and lowered my lips over it.

And he didn't stop me. But, feeling the hardness of his rod in my mouth, it was only minutes before I was throbbing and my body wanted to be buried in his. I raised my head and found his willing lips and pushed him over.

He fell gently back, but then he let out a piercing cry that froze me, even in the heat I was in, and he slapped me hard on the head while he yelled. "Stop, stop. Ahhhh."

I sat up in horror; sure I had scared him, "Sorry I wasn't . . ." But I knew I had been about to take him. Well sort of, maybe.

He sat up panting and started reaching about, "There's a stick or something poking up. Christ, I thought I'd got stabbed. It bloody hurt," he said, feeling about in the rotting grass.

"I think we need to get out of here," I declared, totally confused now.

He struggled up, oohing and aahhing as bits of twig stuck into him and were pulled out of him, and struggled gingerly in the pile of rubbish, hardly able to move. His cock and balls were swinging freely and moving more than anything except his waving arms. The hurt one certainly didn't seem restricted, I even noticed. He seemed totally unconcerned, but it was sending me into heat and even more confusion. Did he want me looking at him, was he so naïve he didn't realize what I was feeling? I had no idea.

"You need pants and shoes," I said. The way he was flailing about naked even looked painful. Sure, it was erotic too, but not with the accompanying yelps, as things stuck into him and he moved his hurt arm the wrong way.

"In the barn," he said, "On the floor. That's a really good idea."

I struggled out of the mess of rubbish and old grass clippings and around to the other end of the barn, muttering to myself. The two big doors were securely padlocked, but the small service door in one of them hung open, and I went inside.

The barn was dry and still, with some abandoned broken-down machinery lying about covered in a heavy layer of dust like the floor was. But in places the dust had been disturbed, and I had no trouble finding Ty's backpack and the neat pile of folded clothes beside it. I grabbed his pants and shoes, but left his briefs there. He'd manage, I thought. And it meant less to take off him later I also thought deep down in my subconscious.

When he had struggled into the clothes and boots, he staggered gingerly out of the rubbish and long grass, then looked at me in confusion before striding around the barn and going inside it. I'd grabbed up my own pack and tagged along behind him.

The shock was wearing off for both of us, and I was feeling mildly embarrassed by my earlier attempt to take him, and he now seemed embarrassed at my presence. But when I joined him inside, he had on a pair of glasses and had produced a bottle of Yellowtail Shiraz from his backpack.

"Drink?" he asked, looking at me as if he was inspecting me, as he opened the bottle and then pulled out a plastic cup, which he filled and handed to me.

"Cheers," I said, downing half the cup of wine in one go. I needed it.

He took a slug straight from the bottle, as I shoved the cup at him, "Here," I said, "We can share," But immediately I had second thoughts, and stopped and said,

77

"Um . . . You aren't, um, that wasn't why was it, because you have . . ."

He looked at me, waiting.

"You haven't got AIDS have you?" I finally managed to say, "That isn't why you jumped, is it?"

He threw his head back—God, what a beautiful neck he had—and laughed. "No. Christ. My excuse is even more boring and common. I . . ." He paused, then looked down at his feet and gulped some more wine down. "I got dumped," He said, "Because I was too old, oh, and what he didn't say, that I'm not a woman."

"Oh," I said, it sounded far too complicated for me just then, but I couldn't stop myself saying, "You looked like a golden angel up there, or a god. When I came out of the bush and first saw you standing in the window."

He looked at me over the mouth of the bottle and took another drink. While the other hand, the one not holding the bottle, ran absently through the hair on his chest, and I almost choked, as I could feel his skin just watching him. And my erection was getting uncomfortable.

"And you're certainly not a woman," I added, trembling as I watched a few drops of red wine run down his chest and get lost in the growth there. "Which is a very good thing. I wouldn't have stopped to watch you if you were. I'd just have kept on hiking and wouldn't have seen you fall," I said, and knew it was true, and thought how awful that would have been to pass someone by like that.

He looked at me seriously. "You wanted to fuck me, didn't you?" he said, "Outside in that pile of stuff."

"Um. Yes," I replied. "I hope that . . ."

"Why?" He asked, "I'm not good looking, I'm too old, and I just jumped out of a barn window trying to kill myself."

"Um. Yes, you are a bit . . . But I still want to, and I think you are incredibly attractive and just the perfect age,"

I said. Being completely honest, as I didn't have any idea what else I could say.

"Garth told me I was too old and no good in the sack," He said, looking at me suspiciously.

"Maybe he was wrong," I reminded him.

He looked at me speculatively. "Oh." Then he looked down at my package, "Do you still want to . . .?" He asked quietly, as he waved an arm, the good one, at the floor.

I looked at the floor. I looked at him. "What a stupid question. And I've got a sleeping bag," I said, as I hurried to pull it out of my backpack before he changed his mind.

He was obviously nutty as a fruitcake, but I had been lusting for him from the first moment I set eyes on him standing high up in that window, arms spread and ready to jump. And nothing since had made me want him less. I was spreading my zipped open sleeping bag out into a flat rug when he produced another one from his backpack.

"I have this one too," he said shyly, as he handed it to me.

I quickly laid them out and then just walked up to him and unzipped and dropped his pants down and wrapped my arms about him and planted my mouth on his, as I rubbed my package against his gorgeous cock.

He fell into the kiss nervously, and after a brief embrace, fiddled with my shirt buttons. I had my hands massaging his butt cheeks as he undid the first one. He was going hard nicely, his veiny cock growing and rising up against my belly, but I unzipped myself and let myself free, in case he never got that far. He was going so slow with the buttons, and I was aching to do him.

I took control then in desperation, driven mad by the way he moved his hands ineffectually about, touching my face, my shoulders and hugging me briefly. Now I pushed him down on the sleeping bags and kept pushing him back, kissing him until he was lying flat on his back. "Just where I wanted you," I thought, looking along his pale well-muscled body and gazing into his blue eyes. Then I knelt back between his thighs and in one smooth movement took his legs in my hands and spread them wide, going down on what he had between his legs. A nice-sized cock, a hairy ball sac I'd have loved to explore further, if I hadn't been obsessed with pushing his legs back toward his sides so my mouth could keep up its explorations and discover his hole.

"Hmmmm," I sighed, feeling his puckered rim wink at me as my tongue found it.

"Oh baby, you are beautiful," I murmured to him, "Just hold your legs there," I instructed, and he fumbled about, making odd grunting sounds.

I stroked my tool briefly, as I stroked my other hand up and down inside his thighs and ran my fingers over his entrance, making it wink again at me. I lifted his butt, and he rolled over more so that I had perfect access to his hole for my mouth.

"Mmm. Beautiful," I reminded him as I bent to run my tongue over it and then around it. He was moaning now and his bud twitching.

I kissed it, and he groaned, and I teased it with my tongue, and he whimpered, and I looked up and saw that his eyes, behind the glasses, were fixed on what he could see happening. My mouth at his hole, my hand on his cock, stroking it, and my other hand pulling at his rim. Then I had my tongue inside him.

"Oh god, yes," he suddenly cried out, "Fuck me. Pump me. Oh god, I want a cock inside me. Do it, do it. Oh, god."

His sudden wild shouting drove me wilder with frustration and desire. I slobbered over him and added a wet finger, and then he was as ready as I had time to get him. I briefly pressed two fingers into his loosened hole. "Oh, god. Now, now take me." He yelled, moving his hips against my hand, driving my fingers deeper. And I was more than ready to oblige him but had to stop to rip open and put on a condom I had got out earlier.

Now he was trying to get my cock into him, reaching for it, moaning, "Yes, oh what a beauty, oh how hard."

We were both guiding it to his entrance, which just seemed to open up and suck me in as he arched his back and moaned wildly, rocking his body about from side to side, twisting himself around my tool as it drove deeper into his channel and I took possession of him.

I cried out, "Oh god, baby," at the way his channel was turning on my throbbing tool as his walls caressed it. I hardly had time to plow him half a dozen times slowly before I was pounding his ass in a frenzy and cumming, giving a cry of release as I did, which I hadn't done for years.

And I thought, "Thank the fuck you are gone, Lachlan." The bastard I'd been keeping for eight years had walked out six months before after telling me he was embarrassed to tell his friends what I did for a living.

"You have the mind of a frustrated housewife," He had thrown at me. "And it's humiliating that you call reading and publishing that romance rubbish a job."

I loved my work, and I had screamed at him how he was never embarrassed about helping to spend what it earned me. "And you are a worse fuck than any bloody romance starved housewife, Lachlan," I'd added, because sex had not been that great for a couple of years.

Now I sagged back, spent, and just looked down at the beautiful sight of my cock disappearing into Ty's ass and stroked his cheeks. But my other hand had joined his on his own tool, and I was looking in his eyes again as he came up his belly and spattered cum on his chest and face. I leant forward and licked it off him, and we fell into a deep kiss. A tongue feeding inside his mouth, as my dick hummed inside his passage. I wasn't leaving his ass till I had come again and only pulled out long enough to get another condom.

After that deep, possessing kiss, he began to move his hands all over me and himself easily, stroking, pinching, tugging. And when he could get his mouth to me, he was licking and kissing me.

When I was recharged, I rode him long, and slow, and deep. And I stroked his nice thick tool as he moaned and writhed and came twice for my once, the last time shooting the little bit of cum he had left up his belly as I came inside him. We lay there connected, cock in ass. Then when I slipped out, hand to cock and hand to cock for some time until he began to fuck my fist. He was young and virile.

"Again," he whispered in my ear,

"Hey, I am not as young as you," I said, as he began to stroke me.

Instead, I moved down, finally having time to wash and explore every bit of his lovely thick cock and his hairy balls with my mouth as he wrapped and unwrapped his legs from around me and ran his hands over his chest and belly, joining my own exploring ones and finally gripping my hair in his fists as he unloaded into my throat.

When I had swallowed his cream, I came up for air, and kissed him. And sitting up, I said honestly, "I think you are an animal in the sack."

He seemed happy and looked half asleep, and in a few minutes I had drifted off too.

In the morning I woke to his hands stoking my erection, and I happily rolled him on his belly and, grabbing another condom, fucked up into him as he lay there nice and tight under me. Him groaning and moving his hips as he rubbed his own dick off on the sleeping bag. He grunted as he came and then rotated his butt for me as I fucked him wildly and came.

"That was the last condom," I said, as I rolled off him, "Unless you have any?"

"No," he said turning to look at me. "I could be fucked by you all day," he added shyly. "Would you want . . .?"

"If I was able," I said laughing and cuddling up close to him in the suddenly chilly morning air, and we wrapped our arms about each other and went into a deep kiss.

HEATING UP YOUR OFFICE

Your office has a glass wall overlooking a staircase that winds up the outside of the building. Beyond the stairs is a cluster of old houses and in between are several large trees that in summer provide greenery and shade and increase your privacy. Now that it is winter the trees are all bare, and you are exposed to the sight of the people in those buildings and to the cold that comes in through the glass.

You are very exposed at your desk and need to warm up. I have brought you a blow heater as I am worried about you getting a chill, and I plug it in and then bend down to put it under your desk, positioning it just right as you laugh and tell me that I am making a fuss, before I turn it on full.

Then you are sighing with pleasure at the heat. You are now even more pleased to see me and in a while your office is warming nicely. Everyone else is leaving for the day, trooping past on the staircase as they leave, some waving to you as they pass.

"Warm enough?" I ask.

"Yes," you say.

I come behind you and catch your arms and run a cord about them.

"Hey," you say, laughing, "what are you . . . ?"

I bend over you and land my mouth on yours, stopping your talk.

I tie the cord off as we kiss.

Then I pull you up so you are standing and push you forward over the desk. Papers fly off as you try to move aside, but now you discover that while I was down under the desk arranging the heater, I had tied each ankle loosely to a leg of your desk. Now you fall forward helplessly.

"What are you doing?" you hiss, the glass wall exposing you to anyone passing. Exposing you well, as your ass is turned slightly to the window. I stay silent, smiling and slowly pull down your pants, then your briefs.

"Not here," you hiss, "Oh no, not here."

The office is lovely and warm now. And I am very overheated, as are you, little beads of sweat starting to break out on your bare skin. Everyone has left and the stairs are empty. A shame, I think. But in the houses opposite, people are coming home now.

You hear my zip go, and then I have a hand under you, feeling your growing appreciation of my intentions. I push your shirt up, running my hands under your body, sliding them over your pecs, your nipples, your belly, turning your face to mine for a kiss as I cup and tug at your balls and then grasp and stroke your almost-full erection. My own erection is pressing into your tied hands and against your lower back. You move your fingers over my cock head, making me jump, and break the kiss. I stroke myself between your tied hands as you grasp at me, sending shivers through me. And I feel you hard and ready, so I rise off you and sit back in your chair, rolling in between your thighs. My hands spread your cheeks to fully expose you, and I begin to open the portal into the smooth, walled tunnel inside you that you so enjoy having well filled.

"Are you warm enough?" I ask. Releasing your cheeks, hiding you.

"Yes, yes," you reply. Your voice shaky. "Don't stop," you add very quietly, pretending not to say it.

"Good," I say.

I spread your cheeks again and bend to bring my mouth to your crinkled rim. You moan the instant my tongue slides over it. I like that sound and intensify my efforts, working the point of my tongue in as you jerk and moan. Then I slide in my thumb, still spreading your cheeks wide with my fingers, then push in the other thumb, and with one buried on each side, I pull at your entrance as I lick and dip into it feverishly.

You whimper at the way I am stretching you, but loosen up almost immediately. I moan in appreciation. Seeing that where I am going to bury my throbbing cock is now gaping from my attentions is driving me wild. I can't wait any longer and, directing myself to that opening, I press my cap to it. My thumbs are still pulling it apart but slip out as my cap pops in. I lean forward over you, a hand on my cock guiding it as I kiss along your back to your neck, nibbling higher as I sink deeper into your welcoming passage.

ILLEGAL DRILLING

The crime rate was pretty low in our part of Adelaide.

My company's head office occupied two professionally restored Edwardian brick houses, set back from a busy six-lane road and sitting next to each other in an old garden. In spite of our central location, the two buildings were an oasis of quiet.

The modern glass extension at the rear of the main building, which housed the administration offices and the boardroom, gave me a spacious office overlooking the back garden. The garden was small but always immaculate, with a perfect half circle of lawn, some climbers over the big corrugated-iron storage shed beyond it, and an old leaning fig tree hanging over a well-placed wooden bench.

Not bad, I thought, looking up from my computer screen and viewing the bench. Not bad at all.

In business there's nothing better than an optimistic budget that's being realized. And that was what I now had before me on the screen. And the wooden bench situated only yards away from me through the floor to ceiling glass reminded me of Arnold. Working back on long summer evenings had its advantages, and Arnold's willingness to lie back over anything and have his ass mined had always been the principal one. I could even now see him draped over the back of the wooden bench, moaning, as I drilled deep inside his tight access shaft, set between the round hills of his bubble butt. There sure was gold in them thar hills, I thought. My white creamy gold. Shame he was out bush exploring for the real thing at the moment. I sighed and returned to my forecasts.

At the very rear of the block, behind the shed, was a cream-gravelled parking area, and I'd vaguely noticed a white van driving in as I'd looked back at my spreadsheets. There was plenty of room in the car park. I knew that most of the staff had already left for the weekend as the big boss was off at our mine site. So, being a summer Friday afternoon, it was a race to leave and get to the beach or head off down the coast for the weekend.

I had an empty house to go back to or some really good figures to massage into a glowing report for Monday's month-end meeting. So I was happy to hang about finishing it off and putting in a bit more effort than I would have with Arnold about. By now he'd be waiting to be driven home for his early evening fuck, or be ready to be fucked at the office if we had the place to ourselves—an advantage of us both working for the same small company.

I was briefly distracted by two guys walking past, through the garden, and turning off to the back door of the other house, which was the main office for the exploration team. Shortly after, they reappeared and came around to the rear entrance of my building. I may not have taken much notice earlier, but now I certainly couldn't help seeing how good they both looked as they entered the sparsely furnished, open-plan rear office. Both were wearing white muscle Ts and long dark shorts, the white setting off their deep, even golden tans and the well-defined muscles of their shoulders and arms.

One smiled broadly at me, and I realized that I didn't recognize either of them and it was a bit late for visitors. I got up and went out to meet them, wondering vaguely if anyone was still inside the other building.

"Hi," I said, "Can I help you?"

"Sure hope so," the taller, more muscular of the two replied. "Have you got a key for the building next door? We came to pick up some tenement maps, but there doesn't seem to be anyone in there."

I was taken aback by the question. The trouble with working in a small mining company is that exploration staff come and go at odd times, and also that being in the admin building and working in the Adelaide office all the time, I never even saw half of them. I was annoyed.

"There's no one there?" I asked.

"No," the two of them replied in unison.

"Well, we're closed now," I said. "So you will have to come back Monday. There is usually someone there from 7:30, or if it's urgent, you can ring Dave Parmenter at home. Have you got his number?" I asked, wondering where I had it written down. I never had any reason to call him.

"It's kinda urgent," the taller one replied. "We're flying up there tomorrow and need those maps."

It came to me finally that for some reason they didn't really look like our field staff. For one thing our geologists always wore khaki on the job. The boss was old fashioned and liked it. I had rarely seen anyone come to the exploration office in anything else.

"I'm sorry," I said, now wary, "I can't help you. You'll just have to come back on Monday. I'll see you out," I added making a move toward them and the back door, which I was now kicking myself for not having locked earlier.

The shorter one moved in behind me as I passed him and stood close. "You here alone?" he asked in a quiet voice that instantly made me freeze up.

It wasn't that he said it threateningly; it was just where he stood and said it, and the situation, that made it frightening.

"No," I stammered suddenly panicking, "Um, no. Someone is coming back soon." I'd hesitated too long trying to think straight for my excuse to sound true, but I carried on helplessly. "That's what I'm waiting for."

"Oh, so who's that?" the tall one asked.

My mind was blank as I opened and closed my mouth silently, looking for inspiration. I couldn't right then think of anyone who might come back. "Tony," I finally said. "Tony forgot something."

"I think he's lying, Dene," the taller one said, smiling broadly and showing perfect white teeth.

"Are you lying?" the short one, Dene, who was standing behind me, asked.

I could smell Dene he was so close, and he smelt good. He looked good too—they both did, and I thought, hey, they shouldn't be doing this to me. Dene looks too nice to be doing this.

"I think you should leave," I stammered and made to move to the door with some vague idea of making a run for it.

"No," I cried in fright as Dene grabbed my elbows from behind and pulled them back, pressing his body against my back and his legs against mine. I was panting, high on an adrenaline rush of fear, ultra aware of him, and shocked to feel his drill was rigid and pressing against my butt.

I struggled against the strong fingers biting into my arms as he held them, but I couldn't help doing it halfheartedly, overwhelmed by the coolness of the two of them.

"Sure looks like he's lying," said Dene, and I felt his hot breath against my neck as he spoke; his face was so close to me.

The tall nameless man stepped toward me, smiling, and I could feel Dene's hot breath suddenly on the side of my face.

"What do you want?" I asked, in a squeaky frightened voice that sounded nothing like mine.

"Luke just wants the key to next door," Dene replied calmly, "You tell us where the spare is and we take it and go away and leave you alone. Now if you don't give us the key . . ."

Luke smiled at me and cracked the knuckles of his big hands, working the muscles in his arms at the same time.

"You can't be serious," I said shakily.

"The key," Luke said, stepping closer, suddenly backhanding me across the face so that I was momentarily stunned.

"In the cupboard over there," I blurted out in a rush, completely overwhelmed by what was going on and feeling utterly helpless.

"Thank you," Luke said politely, as he went to get it.

I expected Dene to let me go once Luke had the key, but instead he held me just as tight. And as Luke came back, I felt Dene stroking his drill up and down between my cheeks and tried to pull away.

"Bring me something to tie him up with," Dene said, holding me firmly. Luke looked around the office.

"Nothing here," he said, frowning; then he reached into his pocket and pulled out a hank of thick cord. "Now what do have I here?" he added, holding it up and smiling.

He joined Dene behind me, and they tied my arms together at the wrists and elbows, running the cord on around my body so it held my arms close in.

When they were done, Dene said, "Come on; time for some exercise," pushing me forward and laughing.

I was in a state of paralyzing confusion and fear. Incapable of saying anything as they led me out of the office building and toward the corrugated-iron storage shed. They opened the side door, and the heat inside hit me like a wave. It had been a hot day, and the closed shed had soaked up the heat and hung on to it. A film of sweat instantly jumped out on my skin.

"Hot," Dene muttered behind me.

Inside, the shed it was dark, but Luke found the light switch and the fluorescent lights flickered into life, giving the place a stark brightness. Then Luke moved over to the pyramid-shaped steel pipe frame standing off in one corner with a big chain operated pulley mounted at its apex. The geologists had used it back in the early days of the company when the exploration team did a lot of their vehicle and equipment maintenance themselves.

"Well, well, how very convenient," said Dene, pushing me toward the frame as Luke played with the pulley chains, raising and lowering the big steel hook that was suspended there.

I was guided under the frame, and the chain sling hanging from the hook was run around me at my chest and waist and rehooked, holding me tight.

Luke pulled the pulley chains, and I was tipped forward and raised up so that I had to stretch to keep my toes on the ground.

I was stuttering, "What are you doing? Let me go. Please," as Dene reached around and undid my belt, then unzipped me.

As I struggled uselessly and asked repeatedly, "Why are you doing this to me?" Dene pulled my pants down to my ankles, then my briefs, before jerking my shoes off and stripping the clothes from my legs. I tried to kick at him but had no leverage and swung about uselessly.

He laughed and pushed a big hand between my thighs and gripped my balls from behind. I yelped and stopped kicking as he squeezed them painfully tight.

In front of me Luke was playing with the chains still, adjusting the height of my torso as Dene pulled one of my feet out to the side and tied it off to one of the frames supports.

"Just about right," Luke said, smiling and looking down at me.

I lifted my head back enough to see up into his face, and in his lowered eyes and half smile I saw something I recognized, it was the same look I'd occasionally glimpsed in a mirror when I was stiff and throbbing and ready to pound Arnold's ass hard.

"Yep, looks good from here too," Dene added, his strong hands spreading my cheeks.

"No," I gasped, shaking my body against the chains and cords that immobilized me.

"Oh, yes," Dene said laughing as his palm hit my butt cheeks.

"Hey, you can't do this," I choked out. "No, no you can't. Let me go, I've given you the key. You promised," I yelled at them as Luke dropped his shorts and kicked them off.

He'd had nothing on under them, and the big mushroom-capped drill he now stroked was bouncing about in front of my face. Then he gripped my hair with one hand and his tool with the other and forced the cap to my lips, rubbing it over them, pushing at me. I twisted and grunted, refusing to open for him, but behind me Luke reached through again and squeezed my balls hard. I opened my mouth to yelp and Luke was inside it. He laughed as he pushed himself to the back of my throat, choking me.

Behind me Dene had taken hold of my other leg and tied it off to another steel pole leaving me spread wide. I was helpless. My body was suspended, caught between the chain sling and my legs, tied to the poles.

"Now, now," Dene replied huskily, "I bet a nice young guy like you loves to have his ass mined deep by a great big tool like this. Oh yes."

"He is a bloody miner." The thought flashed angrily through my mind. I hated it, but I was getting an erection. I wanted to go limp, but my fear had me hard and ready. It's fear, I told myself, nothing else. But a little voice inside me asked if it might also come from being manhandled roughly by two strong, good-looking men.

Dene applied something cool to my hole, and I shuddered. Then his fingers rimmed and tested me, and I shuddered again, gagging on Luke's cock as he fucked my face.

"He's real tight back here, Luke," Dene grunted as I felt a finger entering me. "I reckon he's the one who likes to do the exploring," he added, as his thick finger assessed the tightness of my hole. "Is that right?"

I didn't answer him. He was right, I was always the fucker. But I didn't answer him. And I doubt he expected any answer. My mouth was too full of cock for me to say anything, and my own drill was beginning to throb for some attention as Dene added a second finger and probed my anal shaft deeper.

The shed was hotter and stuffier than ever, and sweat ran down my body and dripped on the grease-stained concrete floor. I was helpless in a nightmare I couldn't wake myself up from. And I knew there was no one outside, no one who would hear me yelling and come to rescue me.

I swayed on the chain, rocking as Luke pulled my head back and forth, fucking my face. I was choking, but short of trying to bite his tool off, there wasn't much I could do, and behind me something even thicker was trying to enter my tunnel. I managed to scream around Luke's huge equipment, because whatever Dene was working into me finally made it through my entrance. He rotated it, intimately exploring the walls of my drive while I shuddered and bucked, chocking on Luke's tool as it muffled my screams.

"I think he likes that wrench handle," Luke grunted as Dene fucked my ass with whatever he had inside me, and my tunnel quivered as I was swung back and forth from Luke's cock, which was hitting the back of my throat. Dene's toy was going ever deeper. I was bucking like a lunatic and widening my ass as much as possible as the tool inside there started me quivering and cumming in spite of my screams.

They swung me back and forth like a doll for what seemed like forever, and my passage stretched, and soon, in spite of the pain, I was moaning as I quivered and spasmed.

Luke swung me back and forth, faster and faster, before pushing me off him and coming in my face. He rubbed his cum in as Dene removed whatever he had been fucking me with from my hole. I felt gutted when it was leaving me, and it slurped coming out.

"He's got a real nice gaping hole now," Dene chuckled, and I had no doubt I did.

He explored my stretched passage with some new piece of ass-mining equipment. This one was easier for me to take, and he had me moaning as he stroked its bulbous end repeatedly over my prostate. Luke reached under me and gripped my own swinging tool.

"Oooh, eee, well this is a big piece of drilling equipment you've got here, a real big bore drill." Luke laughed.

He barely did anything before I again shot repeated bursts of juice over the floor. I was frightened and humiliated, but all my body wanted to do was moan and buck and shoot my seed.

Then Luke was behind me, undoing my legs, and for a few moments I thought he might be going to let me go and relaxed, going with the deep fucking Dene was still giving me. But instead of letting me go, he pulled that leg to join the other, which he released and pulled up and over. My body rotated around Dene's tool without his fucking rhythm changing. I wriggled and arched at the feel of that big-headed tool rotating inside me; then my torso rotated so I was on my back. I could see now that Dene was fucking me with his own tool, or rather I was fucking myself on him as he pulled me back and forth.

Luke stood behind him, and his hands wrapped around and played over Dene's chest and belly as they kissed. I could see Dene's cock going in and out of me, and with the sight of them kissing, I was recharging rapidly. Luke noticed.

"I couldn't hear this guy scream before; make him do it again," he said to Luke, watching me from where he was cuddled up behind his mate.

I whimpered in fear. There was some whispering and laughing. Then they broke their embrace.

Dene slipped out of me and, I saw his glistening bulbous-headed cock for the first time. Each of them took one of my legs and walked it forward, lifting my hips as they moved to tie me to the other two poles, the ones past my head. I was more uncomfortable, partly doubled over, but Luke played with the chains, adjusting the level of my torso and butt.

Dene slipped right back in, and Luke went behind him and I screamed and lurched. Luke was working something inside me, right under Dene's cock. Dene yelled almost as loudly as I did as it entered me, and I was rocked back and forth, gently at first, then faster and faster, my yells and Dene's mingling until I was flooded. Dene withdrew, and I whimpered with relief, but then a smiling Luke moved in and, yelping and grunting, fed his huge tool in above the small handle still buried inside me. I had stretched under the earlier abuse, but this time it was almost unendurable. The fucking was only brief before Luke emptied himself inside me. He stayed buried, but the handle was removed, leaving me gaping and quivering and exhausted. Dene came up to my head and tilted it back and just slid his stiff tool straight in and down my throat. I gagged just as he pulled back and he fucked my face deep and long as Luke rehardened inside me.

"I think it's time I lubricated you again," Luke said as he began exploring my shaft again.

I grunted unwillingly for him, unable to stop myself. Soon I was again rocking back and forth between the two of them, shooting my load yet again, up over my belly and chest. Luke came again and withdrew, and as he did, I felt some of the cream they had both left behind dribble out along my crack.

"Ooo eee," Luke said, "you are open and dripping. A beautiful sight," he added, rubbing the cream back between my cheeks.

Dene buried himself in my throat and jerked a couple of times, flooding me with his cum. "Oh, yes." He moaned.

Then they were gone and the door of the shed closed with an ominous clang.

I hung there, aching and sore, sweat running off me and cum dripping out of me.

Then Luke was back. "I'll just leave you with something to keep you ready," he said. "Now just so your tunnel stays wide open, ready for me to explore when I come back, I'm going to leave you with this." He slid a short piece of metal pipe inside me. In the position I was in, I couldn't do anything but look at the end of it poking out of my ass and hope it popped out. When he'd gone, I tried pushing it out but it just sank in a fraction further, stretching me more.

Outside I could hear some activity, and eventually there was a loud thump, presumably as something heavy was loaded into their van. My thoughts turned from my own nightmare situation to my employer's possible losses. There was a lot of valuable equipment in the Exploration office, and I also knew that all of it was well insured. But I realized that there was also a lot of highly sensitive and valuable data kept there that might be worth money to someone if they really knew what they were looking for.

My mind raced around in circles wondering what Dene and Luke might be stealing that was worth the risk they were taking; after all, I could identify both of them.

Well, I could if I was still alive, I realized, suddenly going cold. Whatever Luke had sunk in my shaft was starting to make my tunnel's muscles quiver, and I was lost between my own drill beginning to harden up again and the potential damage Luke and Dene could do to me. I wriggled and squirmed, suddenly desperate to get away. But I soon had to admit that the way they had tied me up meant I couldn't do anything.

When they returned, Luke removed the section of pipe from my gaping hole and Dene pulled my hips back toward him. They took turns mining my gaping hole and exploring my throat. And I let them do it without saying anything, too afraid of what might happen to me if I annoyed them. I was soon hard and throbbing too, moaning as loudly as they did and mindlessly pumping my hips in time with their fucking.

Dene's huge drill reamed me out for ages before he came. Then Luke plunged his own tool back inside for another bit of rough exploration, this time assisted by Dene's thick fingers, just to make my entrance again feel as if it was going to tear apart. When they had both finished with me, their cum was again dribbling out of my ass. Finally, they moved away, talking quietly to each other as they left me, and I heard the shed door open and close, leaving me suspended in silence. Outside I heard their van leave the parking lot and disappear.

It was Friday night on a summer weekend that was forecast to have a heat wave, and it was already hot and stifling inside the corrugated-iron shed. My whole body ached, and soon tears of fear and helplessness began to drip onto the floor under me, joining the sweat and cum already darkening the oil-stained concrete.

I was a mess by the time I heard noises outside, a vehicle coming in to the car park and stopping. In my terror I had no idea who it was. It didn't sound like their van, but I was hoping they had come back to let me go, though I was terrified they would come back for some other reason.

Then the shed door opened. "Help," I croaked fearfully, not able to see if it was Dene or Luke coming back, or someone else. "Who is it?" I said haltingly as footsteps came closer.

Suddenly cool fingers were at my ass and I was being rimmed by a cool tongue. It was a relief for my hot, sore, abused hole but also torture as I knew they were back to abuse me again.

"No," I said, then louder, "No, no, no," I screamed as I shook my body with as much strengths as I could muster, trying to dislodge the hard fingers and tongue from my ass.

"Ok. OK." a voice said. "Jeez, Dave, settle down."

"Arnold," I cried, "Arnold, oh god," I sobbed, as a wave of relief overcame me. "Oh god."

He didn't seem to move, and I tried to swing around to see him, beginning to wonder why he wasn't getting me out of the position I was in.

"Hey, you did enjoy it, didn't you?" he asked hesitantly.

"Get me down," I begged, desperate to be out of there. "Arnold, get me down."

"I mean, you said you had fantasized about being raped," he was saying.

"What?" I said, not following him, "Robbed, we've been robbed, and they tied me up . . . and, just get me down please."

"You did like it, didn't you?" he asked again.

"Arnold, get me out of here," I cried, throwing myself about in panic, I wanted to get out of that shed and my nightmare.

Arnold finally untied my legs and lowered me to the ground, where he unhooked and untied my arms and body. I was shaking with relief and fear all mixed up together.

"Uh, are you OK?" he asked, uncertainly wrapping his arms round me as I leaned against him.

"No, I am not," I gasped back, clutching at him. "Go and ring the police, Arnold. Just ring the police," I said, feeling him standing there, hesitating.

"What are you waiting for?" I demanded looking at him.

"Uh, well, I thought you would like to live out your fantasy. I mean getting tied up and raped is your favorite one."

Things were starting to fall into place in my fear-riddled mind.

"This had something to do with you?" I asked, as my mind got around what he had been saying. "Dene and Luke. You know them?" I added uncertainly, starting to feel angry.

"Yes, they are doing some contract work for us. They are really into domination and bondage. So . . ." Arnold had the decency to hesitate, "Well, so it seemed like a good idea. They said you would enjoy it. I mean . . . it is your fantasy."

I looked at Arnold as what he said registered fully, then in a mindless rage I threw myself at him, wrestling him to the ground. I ripped down his khaki shorts and somehow got my great big throbbing drill inside his tight hole and drove it in and out of him like a battering ram. He squealed and pawed at the rough concrete trying to escape, yelling at me to stop, until the pleasure overcame the pain and he was shouting for me to go harder.

I did go harder, so hard he was soon yelling again and beating at the concrete floor with his fists. And God I enjoyed it.

INTERRUPTION TIME

I stand in the doorway and watch my lover sitting there. He looks busy, engrossed, as he usually does. I smile because he hasn't heard me arrive and I like to see him unaware like that. I am buzzing. My cock is buzzing, tantalizingly thinking about him, about his body, his flesh mobile under my hands. Thinking about my body exploring his warm internal spaces. I move my hand to my filling cock and stroke over it as I move in to him. I stand behind him, and he still doesn't know I am there he's so engrossed. I reach out my hands and make contact at his shoulders, running them down his chest as he jumps, startled.

"You frightened me," he says, laughing.

"Will I go?" I ask, not wanting to, pinching his nipples, my hands now back there after having glided down and up his firm torso.

"No," he says, relaxing back in his chair. "No," he says again as I turn his chair around and bend my head to take his mouth with mine. His hands are on my hips moving across my ass, I reach for the lift lever and lower his seat.

He is breathing heavily now because he knows I'm going to fill him soon. Give him just a small taste of what I am looking forward to doing to him tonight when we climb into bed together.

I am leaning over him as he slips off my pants and I spring free for him. I unzip him, and he lifts his ass for me to pull his pants off him. Then I kneel down as he slides his ass forward and together we arrange his thighs wide and up over the chair arms. I love it when he presents himself to me like that. He is scrunched up, but his lean, flat belly curls and creases nicely, a rippled bed for his hard cock.

"Fuck me," he says quietly, his eyes fixed on mine, his hands caressing me.

"So you want my cock in here?" I say smiling. Then I'm biting his nipple as I plunge two wet fingers inside his ass.

"Yes," he gasps, as I nibble his other nipple softly, while I move my fingers inside him as he likes me to. I withdraw them and find his mouth again; he pulls me in to him eagerly, hungrily. My cock knocks his, slides against his, dances with his. I run my hand down and hold them together, briefly, as I take his mouth. His hands knead my shoulders until I let go and unbend.

I kneel and take my cock in my hand and watch as I move the head up and down from his asshole to his sac, circle his hole, wetting it, and then moving gently up, stroking him. He is looking at me; I could drown in his eyes when I am starting to make love to him. Then his hands are moving on my arms; then he's touching himself. I like to see him touch himself a bit. I arrive back at his hole and press in. I am wet and I slip in the first bit easily. He moves his hips to me as he does always. He likes me inside him so much, wants my cock filling him, living inside him, warm and alive and occupying him, connecting us inside and outside.

He locks on my eyes and I smile at him as he takes me. He smiles back briefly. Then I am fucking him as he holds himself open for me, there in his office chair. I ride him in slow, long strokes, loving the tightness that encloses me. When he starts to moan, I look at him hazily, lovingly, seeing his eyes closed for a moment. He's lost in his softly moving body rocking to my motion while caressing me. Connected and joined, sharing the pleasure of his flesh.

It's long and slow. A timeless lazy afternoon as he moans and sighs, shivers and arches his body, rocking on a wave of sensual fucking motion. I join him, moving to the same swell until I fill him with my liquid, overflowing from me in a great, arching shudder. He's stroked himself and come too, in a shot of white spray up the shore of his naked rippled belly.

I move in to kiss his mouth one last time. Then I gently lick his salty spray from his warm skin. I kiss his nipples softly because tonight I'll make them burn, kiss his belly, inside which I so love to move my cock, kiss his fingers, his thighs, his soft skin, feel his body hair, brushing it with my lips.

I leave him to do some work so he doesn't complain that I demand too much. I'm humming again, thinking about what I'll do to him tonight.

I VISIT THE ROMAN BATHS

My friend had invited me to join him in the baths. I knew this was a custom of his people and that everyone, men and women, went to the public baths to bathe and talk. And I well knew that much of the men's talk was business. As I wished to do business with his people, I accepted his invitation. But I accepted it with some nervousness, because I had heard stories of things occurring there between the men—things other than talking and bathing.

We arrived at the baths, entering the fine marble building and being made welcome by an attendant who showed us to a place to undress and leave our possessions. I had rarely been naked in front of other men or women before, coming as I did from a cold place where keeping warm was of great importance and cleanliness was not considered much.

My friend and his people were all black-haired, olive-skinned, well-muscled men. I admit that from the first time I had seen them I found them most attractive. Now that I saw my friend naked I was much taken also with the pattern of his black body hair. It curled thickly about his chest, almost hiding the rings of his dark nipples. Then it ran down in a thick column over his flat belly to his . . . ahh, well, I averted my gaze in embarrassment. But there was certainly a profusion of thick black hair there.

As my friend led the way to the baths, I was uncomfortably aware that the sight of him naked had aroused me, and I positioned my hand and walked slightly behind him to hide my state from him and the other men we passed. He had advised me that we would be using a private bath, and I was relieved to know this when I saw how many men there were in and about the main pool. They were of all shapes and sizes, but mainly they were fine, well-muscled men it was a pleasure to set my eyes on. Men who I could not avoid admiring, which increased the obviousness of my embarrassment.

Quite a few men seemed to be watching us as we passed. They were smiling and nodding, and I was glad that my friend was so well known there. But their attention meant that my public erection was embarrassing me more, though I knew I was of a good size and thickness.

We entered a smaller steamy chamber and were greeted by seven well-made men seated in a much smaller pool. My friend introduced me, and we entered the water, with me trying poorly to hide my engorged manhood from these strangers I hoped to do business with.

The water was warm, and I gasped at the sensual feel of it about my manly parts as I lowered myself down on to the seat that rimmed the bath.

Even though these men were strangers I was to do business with, I realized then that I wanted to see their weapons filled and feel them making their way into me and thrusting strongly inside my ass. I had many pleasant memories of summer evenings and nights spent with my fellow tribesmen when hunting in the hills, though we had rarely removed our clothing for such activities. But I doubted my pale skin and lean body, almost hairless in comparison to theirs, would hold any appeal to them with so much young, well-muscled flesh parading about outside.

The strangers were soon looking me over with curiosity and talking to my friend and questioning him about me. He translated some of the questions for me, but I was quickly aware that he was not translating all that was being said.

"My friends find your pale skin and your light hair fascinating. They are asking if they may touch you to see how it feels. Do you mind if they touch you?" my friend asked me at one point.

I was nervous, but also greatly excited by their request to touch my skin and hair. I wished to please these men I wanted to do business with but was already so aroused my organ was standing up straight in front of me. And I was worried what would happen if they touched me, thinking that their hands on me would probably be enough to make me shoot my seed. But I nodded and said shyly, "Of course they may. I can understand their curiosity. They may feel my skin and hair if they wish to."

My friend says something to his friends and they nod and look at me, smiling and laughing, obviously pleased with my answer. I smile nervously as the largest of them moves through the water to me. I am vaguely aware of my friend moving in closer to me before sitting up on the rim of the bath behind me. I feel his legs spread wide about my shoulders and then he is reaching down and lifting my arms up above my head and pulling them back to his chest. The stranger is now before me and my chest is pushed out toward him as he moves between my thighs, his legs pushing them further apart as I moan at the feeling of my friend's growing manhood pressed against my back and neck. The man before me reaches down and takes hold of my throbbing manhood and smilingly speaks. And I know that he is telling his friends that he is pleased with what he now has in his hand.

I try to pull my arms down, but my friend has them tightly gripped and I am trapped. Another man comes over and sits next to me. He runs his hand over my chest, feeling my nipples before running his fingers down to join his friend's in feeling the size and thickness of my throbbing manhood. I gasp at the feel of both men's hands encircling me before one runs his fingers down under my balls and squeezes them lightly as the hand on my manhood begins to stroke me.

The man beside me moves his mouth to mine, and I strain to move my head and free my hands, because this is not something men should do together. But as I can't move away, he takes my mouth with his anyway. In a moment I am gasping, at the stroking my manhood is getting and the way my balls are tugged about, and I've allowed his tongue in my mouth and I am full of it. I decide quickly that I like to have his mouth where it is and move my tongue with his.

Suddenly another man is sitting at my other side and he has grasped my right leg and lifted it up and back toward his chest. His other hand is running under me, under my balls, between my open legs and between my cheeks. I am gasping and moaning about the kissing man's probing tongue and shoot my seed into the water as fingers find my rear entrance and make their way up inside me. The man standing before me strokes my nipples as he talks to his companions. My mouth is released and I see the other men in the bath have their eyes fixed on me as they stroke themselves beneath the water. The man before me reaches down and I feel more fingers enter me behind, spreading me open. I writhe as I am penetrated deeply by thick strong fingers and the man beside groans and begins to rub his own huge engorged cock against the front of my thigh.

I lurch from the deep rubbing and want to come, suddenly moaning and gasping and widening my thighs and lifting my left leg and wrapping it about the man in front's thigh. A mouth has found my nipple and bites it, and I discover that this sends a shudder through me and cry out again and begin to move my hips.

Suddenly, the men lift me bodily and dump me on top of my friend on the lip of the bath, and I feel my friend lie back, taking my stretched arms with him so that I lie extended along the top of his body, his hard weapon now pressing along my spine.

The largest stranger stands up on the seat I have just vacated, and for the first time I see his huge, engorged weapon. I cry out as he moves it in between my spread thighs and his companions grasp my legs and lift and spread them even wider.

I let out an agonized cry as he forces his flared head past my entrance and have tears of pain on my cheeks as he works himself deeper into me. I roll my butt and arch my back both trying to escape him and to ease his entry, gasping and crying out. Another man caresses my belly while his companion pulls at a nipple.

The great tool inside me begins to jerk in and out in small stabs and I cry out again, arching and writhing. A hand squeezes and pulls at my sac, which makes me gasp, as a mouth descends to my growing manhood and engulfs it. I moan and cry out again, realizing that as I was distracted, the great tool has buried itself to the hilt inside my passage. Then it is stroking in and out of me, and I feel a wave of pleasure rush up my body as it caresses my straining, opened passage.

The internal stroking becomes more rapid and pleasurable until I feel my insides flooded with the man's hot seed, and I come into his companion's mouth from the feel of it. As soon as that spent tool is withdrawn another is finding its way inside, to repeat the stroking that I now want so desperately, straining my hips to meet this new man's thrusts, moaning and sighing as another flood fills me.

Each of the seven men sharing the bath with my companion and me enters and fills me so that I feel the cream they have left behind running out of me as each withdraws. When they have each had their turn with me, my friend releases my stretched arms and sits and pulls me up and onto his own throbbing organ, which I ride eagerly in spite of my exhaustion. And I only have to stroke myself briefly till I come for the fourth time, watching the other men about the bath now taking each other lustily.

When I come off my friend's spent tool, the largest of his friends approaches me again and leads me to the wall. I rest forward as he sends his huge manhood snaking slowly deep inside my now well-stretched passage and works it in and out for some considerable time till he fills me again. I have his seed running down my legs as I turn about. But I am not allowed to rest. Another man comes at me and lifts my thigh high and enters me quickly behind as I stand leaning against his companion who has taken my mouth and is rubbing my nipples. I feel his thick engorged manhood and stroke it to greater hardness, preparing him for his coming turn inside me.

It is night when we finally leave the baths, and my friend has a litter come to carry me back to his house, as I have difficulty walking. I spend some days there with him, my time well occupied in becoming closer friends and business associates with those I have already met at the baths, who visit regularly.

KILLING TIME

I had wandered into the bookshop to kill time.

My appointment with Carol at the employment agency was for 11.30 AM, and I had caught the eight o'clock train in from the lake. For once it arrived on time.

The employment agency was on the second floor of the building, and I found the bookshop at street level. I had an hour to fill in before I had to go up, so I thought I'd look for a book I had been after for some time, *The Mycenaeans* by Lord William Taylour. It is an old book, but still the best one about the civilization of the ancient Greeks who lived and died in Homer's Iliad.

Inside the front door was a small counter with a tall, rather patrician-looking man standing behind it. He smiled at me as I wandered in.

"Can I help you with anything in particular?" he asked, not pushily, just helpfully.

"Where would I find the history section?" I replied, and he told me to go through to the back of the shop.

The bookshop was long and narrow, but wide enough to have shelves running across its width as well as along the side walls. Whoever had put the shelving in, though, had apparently wanted people to have privacy to wander. They had not put a tidy straight corridor running from the front of the shop to the back.

Instead, the cross shelves were broken up in different places, almost creating private rooms where you could browse and move on without being seen. I wound up in the rearmost room and began to go through the books on the shelves, finding the ancient history section and narrowing the area of my search down.

"Very nice," a voice said, and I jumped.

I had been concentrating and hadn't heard the man from the front counter arrive. He was standing in the entrance to that room looking me up and down in an odd way.

I acknowledged him with a, "Hi, I found it," wondering if he thought I was trying to steal something.

"Good," he replied, "Would you like me to suck your cock?"

I wasn't sure I had heard right and looked at him in confusion. He moved closer to me. "I would really like to suck your cock. Can I see it?" He was next to me now and pushed me back against the shelves, Roman History, I think it was.

"Umm . . . I think I'd better go," I stammered.

He wasn't bad looking for a mature man—nice cared-for body, streaks of steel gray though this long, dark hair, which was tied back in a short ponytail. I tried to edge away.

He placed a hand on my chest, pushing me back, and I yelped as I felt his other hand land on my crotch. He had me unzipped, with his hand inside, fondling me through my underpants, before I realized what he'd done.

"Hey, Stop that," I yelped, flailing my arms about and trying hard to push him off and wriggle away. "Get your hands off me."

He was surprisingly strong, and I was horrified to feel the hand he had on my cock getting a quick response.

112

"Very nice," he said, smiling. "Get it out so I can see it and I'll let you go."

His voice was quite well educated, and I couldn't believe he was doing this to me.

"You'll let me leave if I show you my cock?" I stammered, thinking that was better than risking messing up my clothes before the interview.

I really wanted the job I was going for and knew I was lucky to have made the first short list.

"That's right," he replied his hand inside my pants having got me hard by now. It was a while since anyone else had touched my cock, and it liked the attention.

"OK," I said, wanting to escape.

I undid my waistband, opened my trousers out, and then pushed my underpants down. His fingers were still around my cock, stroking it.

"You can let go now," I said breathily. I was getting really hard, which was not helping me to be firm with him about letting go.

"Very nice," he said, looking at my dick. "So how long does it get?" he asked, looking at me.

"Eight inches," I replied automatically, always pleased to be able to say that in certain situations. "Now will you let me go?" I protested weakly, making flapping moves to get his hand off me.

I liked women, loved women, but a couple of guys had jerked me off before, and one had even sucked me off, so I wasn't completely averse to the bookshop man's attentions.

"You're enjoying this, aren't you?" he said, smiling broadly as his fingers swished drops of precum around my knob. I wasn't far off eight inches by then.

Now that I'd given up struggling, his other hand moved in on my balls, his fingers slipping under them and teasing them in a very pleasant way.

I let out a moan, thinking vaguely that coming now would leave me relaxed for the interview ahead. I usually got really wound up and nervous and tongue-tied.

He bent down and brought his tongue to my tip, touching it to my slit and tasting me there. Then he ran his tongue down around the shaft and traced it along the big vein before sliding his lips over the end and sucking on it. I groaned and leaned back. I knew I was there till the finish now.

He started to suck me in deeper, and my hands were tangling in his long hair as my hips began to fuck me into his face. He held my butt in his hands now, my pants on the floor, my underpants half way down my thighs. He was doing a good job on me, better than the other guy had.

I was getting ready to come when he stopped, pulling his face off me even though I tried to hold him there. He was surprisingly strong.

"Turn around and bend over," he said looking up, and I saw a trickle of saliva running out at the corner of his mouth.

"No," I said, "finish me, god, please finish me." I moved my own hand to my shaft, but he pulled it back roughly. "I want you bent over with your cute little asshole in my face," he growled, and suddenly I wasn't quite so keen anymore. No one was going there, certainly not some guy who was just about raping me behind the bookshelves.

"No way," I gasped angrily. "You said I could go if I showed you my cock. Well I have, so I want to go now."

He laughed at me and stood up. He seemed to have gotten taller. I tried to pull up my pants, but he forced his knee between my legs and I was trapped. My cock was softening, and I was getting frightened.

"What's going on here?" a voice suddenly cut in.

A wave of relief swept over me as my tormentor backed off, and I looked up to find a guy in running gear standing in the entrance to the room. I struggled with my underwear in embarrassment.

"You're fired, Reg!" the stranger shouted.

"You can't fire me, I run this dump," Reg shouted back angrily, storming off past the stranger and out of that section of books.

"Thanks," I said sheepishly, not quite sure what to say to explain my half-undressed state. "I've got an interview upstairs at 11.30," I babbled. "With Carol. I just came in here to look around."

I tucked my still slightly full, saliva-coated cock into my underpants, noticing a wet patch on them already and bent to pull up my trousers.

"Well, it's a quarter past now and you look a mess. I know Carol well. So, how about I ring her up and we see if she can see you a bit later?" my rescuer said, and I glanced at my watch and saw that he was right. My head was an even bigger mess than the rest of me right then.

"My name's Dave, by the way," he added, smiling.

"Paul," I replied holding out my hand, and we shook.

"So, Paul, come upstairs and I'll call Carol."

He opened a door at the back of the room, which I hadn't really noticed before. "You work here?" I asked

"Yes. It's my bookshop," he replied. "I should probably have sacked Reg ages ago. I have had a couple of complaints. But he knows the stock better than I do." He smiled apologetically. He had a friendly smile.

Upstairs was a big sunny apartment, antique furniture, miles of polished floors. "You live here too?" I said surprised.

"I don't like commuting," he replied, smiling broadly.

He called Carol and said he needed a big favor. Then, after a few minutes chat, which I couldn't really hear, he passed the phone to me.

"Dave says you have had an accident," Carol was saying.

"Yes, I'm really sorry."

"Well don't worry. Come at 12.30 PM. I'll take an early lunch. Hope you're OK."

I was relieved. Now that I was upstairs, I was feeling a bit shaky. Reg had given me quite a fright.

"Why don't you have a shower and get properly tidied up," Dave suddenly said. "I can even lend you some clean underwear if you need it. It's the least I can do in the circumstances."

As I now had another hour to kill, and I was feeling sticky, I took him up on his offer.

I undressed in the bathroom and he came in with a clean towel for me just as I was about to get into the shower. I must have forgotten to lock the door, I thought, embarrassed.

"By the way," he said, and I turned to him. He dropped to his knees and took my still slightly full cock into his mouth.

"Ummm, wha . . . Ummm," I sputtered briefly, but after the earlier work it felt so good and he had saved me after all.

He sucked me in and I was getting hard fast, swelling in his mouth as he stroked me with his magic tongue. I moaned and my hips were soon calling the tune again. I hardly noticed at first that he had a hand at my anus. And I was sighing and moaning too much to do more than note it as he pushed a finger up inside me. When he pushed two in, I was fucking his mouth seriously. Suddenly his fingers moving in my ass were really doing something to me, and I gasped and quivered and fucked his face harder.

I was as big and hard as I could get, and he opened his throat to me and, with what was happening inside my ass and his sucking, god, it was wonderful. I moaned and gasped as I sunk myself in him, my cock quaking as I came,

116

pumping my cum inside his throat over and over, more than I ever did. He swallowed all of it, licking me as I slowly let myself slip out, cleaning me up as I withdrew and slumped back against the outside of the shower stall weak at the knees.

"I think you enjoyed that," he said, looking up at me and smiling.

Then he was standing next to me, his shorts off and his own stiff rod pressed against my belly. He found my mouth with his and my rubbery lips let his tongue inside where he found mine.

I was too weak to do more than go along for the ride, and my head swam aimlessly. He moved a hand back to my asshole as we kissed and soon had his fingers back inside me. I wasn't complaining, he had saved me and given me the greatest head job I'd ever had.

He left my mouth and turned me about ready to go into the shower, I thought, but then I felt his hands on my ass cheeks, parting them, and something firm and wet was working at my hole.

I groaned as he did things to me there that felt way too good to make him stop. I eased my ass back, opening it up instinctively for him. He worked his fingers in again and touched whatever it was he had touched before, making me groan. He emptied me for a moment but then was back smearing something warm about my hole and taking it inside me when his fingers returned there. I moved my ass back further as my cock began to harden noticeably, never having gone completely soft.

I was moaning again and had moved one hand to fist my own cock as his fingers twisted and stroked about inside me, opening me up. I felt a sharp pain as something bigger went in past my entry. Then it was making my ass feel incredibly full and I moved my legs back further and spread them wider to let it fill me deeper. I was half way bent over, leaning my hand and face against the outside of the shower stall.

He emptied my ass for a moment, and I groaned my displeasure to him, having got used to it and liking it.

But he was soon back, parting my cheeks again and pushing something sticky at my entrance.

"Ouch," I cried out, startled, grunting loudly as with a sudden burning pain it penetrated inside me. I gasped it felt so big, and I couldn't believe the way it felt going further inside me. I grunted and pushed back against it, pushing my butt back to take it. It slid in further, making me moan. I spread my legs wider, and I suddenly knew it was his cock. I had a cock up my ass. And god I loved it.

I was shocked at myself but past caring about anything but the full feeling of it and what it was doing inside me. He moved it back and forth, gently stroking at the magic something he had found in there. His hand took over from mine on my own rod and I was glad to be able to use both hands to support my melting body.

"Ohhh," I moaned, "God," I gasped, "Fuck me," I hissed at him. "Deeper. God, I want you deeper."

He obliged me, working his cock deeper into me, filling places I hadn't even known were empty. I writhed under his cock and his hand, as it worked my own cock. I felt his pubes stroke my ass as he bottomed inside me and his balls between us. Then he withdrew what seemed forever before he fucked in deep again. He began to fuck my ass seriously, and I moaned for more.

"Oh god, that is so good," I cried out in a strangled voice. "Oh god, fuck, fuck me faster," I cried, "faster," as his hand on my cock hit the rim of my knob and I felt my gut begin to quiver on his fucking cock.

I felt it come from my balls, my ass going into spasms on him as he planted himself deep and stayed there, and my cock jerked as the first cum let loose. The threads were thick and flying high, hitting my chest and belly and then the glass of the shower cubicle. Another jerk and it hit my belly and the floor, and again, the last of it falling on to the tiled floor.

My ass stopped quivering as he slowly withdrew his cock, leaving me feeling empty and shaky and hardly able to stand, resting all my weight on the glass before me.

Dave nuzzled and nibbled at my neck and stroked my back with firm hands.

"Thanks for the great fuck, Paul," he said gently. "Now you'd better get yourself cleaned up or you'll be late."

I grunted something to him and just hung there, sagging and mindless for some time, totally fucked.

Reg was nowhere to be seen and the front door of the shop was locked when I floated out, clean and fresh and smelling good. I was on time for my revised appointment and didn't have the energy to be nervous. Getting fucked I thought vaguely seemed to be good for my employment prospects.

* * * *

At 12.45 pm at the front counter of the book shop Dave was feeling Reg's dick up, liking the hard smallness of it. "So, next time I'm the bad guy and you get to be the good guy," he said, smiling.

Reg met his lips in a gentle kiss. Pulling away after a few moments, he said, "I know it's me next time. But god, Paul, was cute. You always get to play good guy with the really cute ones."

"Well, Carol's e-mailed the photos of tomorrow's appointments for you to check out, so you just have to hope it's another cute one who comes in here to kill some time."

MOTIVATING THE BUYER

The house was built on a rise, and the garden sloped gently down to the banks of the Hunter River. Willows and reeds lined the shore, and a few ducks busied themselves feeding in the water, occasionally turning their tails up as they lowered their beaks to the muddy bottom. I looked behind me. The house was impressive, a fine Georgian-style home with fifteen rooms, not counting bathrooms or laundry.

It was very pleasant, but so were a lot of other houses. What I needed if I was going to decide to buy this one was some sort of extra inducement: wild salmon or trout in the river, a healthy, artistically inclined community. I needed something more than just a nice building in a convenient location to make any house grab me.

The pavilion was set down near the river to the left of the park-like grounds. Taking in the view from the house, one saw the whole picture, the sloping green lawn with darker old pines at the sides of it, and at the end, the river. And sitting just in front of it on the left was the white, French-inspired pavilion and on the other side a collection of Japanese maples.

The pavilion created a romantic effect with its pointed roof and high, round-topped French windows, opening outward, as they were now, their fine white curtains catching in the breeze and drifting out of them occasionally, adding to the lightness and romance of it. And to the right, in the right season, would be the fiery blaze of Japanese maples. A bit leery for my tastes, but still effective, I imagined. It was summer now and the trees were green.

I wandered down to the pavilion for a closer look. It was octagonal[repetitious], and the windows on the sides facing the river and the park were open. I stepped up into the cool dimness of the interior. Pleasant, I thought.

But for some reason it was furnished in Balinese carved teak furniture, the busyness and darkness of the timber at odds with the lightness and fragility of the pavilion itself. To one side was a canopied day bed, its three sides intricately carved. The cushions were cream and soft looking, and the muslin curtains matched the fabric floating at the French windows. Two lounges cushioned in the same cream fabric faced each other across a full-sized "opium bed" coffee table. And to the side, a small marble-topped Dutch Indonesian reproduction table stood with two matching chairs, again cushioned in cream. An ancient willow-patterned tureen stood on top of it filled with overblown roses, the petals falling artistically on the marble.

The only interior decoration that really appealed to me was the young man sleeping naked on the day bed. I had been encouraged to wander down this way by the real estate agent, Rosemary, who had implied I might find something here to help encourage me to buy the house.

If the dark-haired young man was meant to induce me, well he was certainly appealing to me in the right way now. And he was definitely causing a reaction.

His back was toward me, his firm, rounded butt and full muscular thighs were right there in front of me as I stepped up to the bed.

I bent and kissed each firm round cheek and ran my tongue over them, he tasted fresh, just a hint of salt from the heat of the day.

I ran a hand up over his thigh and along his side to the hidden head, nestled in a pillow cradled in his arms up in the far corner, where the day bed's side and back met. I ran my hand back down to the glossy hair on the back of his thighs and then slipped my fingers between those thighs.

He moved languidly and made little muttering noises as if he was deeply asleep. I slipped my fingers out and was excited by the game. I bent and nibbled and licked his butt cheeks again. Then I continued on, up his muscular back as he moaned, and moved slightly, as if to escape me.

He was a very good actor, I decided. I was leaning over him now and ran my free hand over his hip and down into the hidden mass of his pubic hair, feeling his thick but still-soft cock, and his balls hanging loosely across his lower thigh. The pubic hair was thick, and his cock was already filling out under my exploring hand. Reasonable, I thought, as he moaned in his pretend sleep. I continued to stroke his dick, playing with his cap and the slit, just enjoying the feeling of him stiffening. I was sitting on the edge of the bed now, and my other hand couldn't help moving between his cheeks. I stroked a finger across his hidden entrance. He twitched and seemed to jerk, as if waking suddenly, and then he was pulling his legs away and throwing an arm wildly back at me.

"Hey," he cried. "Who are you?" as he crawled away, across the bed.

I grabbed at his hips and pulled him back to me, as he pretended to try to escape. Now I knelt on the bed straddling his upper thighs, just below his butt, and gripped him tight between my knees. One hand planted itself in-between his shoulder blades and I leaned half my weight there, pinning him down. He stopped struggling as I licked two fingers, and he began moaning as I played them over his hole and pressed into it.

"Who are you?" he suddenly asked again.

"You're a good actor," I said and leaned into him. "Give me a kiss."

The first part of one finger took the first small step to the coming fuck, by passing through his puckered rim. And he turned his face to the side and let his lips meet mine. When our lips finally parted, that finger, and the other, were both buried inside him, to the limit. He had gasped and tried to twist away at first as I moved them in and twisted them, but I had held him fast. Now he was moaning in pleasure. Begging for more.

I let him lift his ass then, and he pushed it back to me and spread his thighs further apart. I removed my fingers and, kneeling on the bed between his spread thighs, bent my head to lick him, as one hand went under and found his flapping, dripping rod and stroked that. I was using the precum to lubricate the helmet with my thumb, while my other hand tugged and rolled his balls. He came in shuddering bursts, spilling his cream out in long arcs over the cream-covered bed.

I returned my fingers to his passage. He moaned and I soon had worked in two from each hand, set at each side, pulling and spreading him so my tongue flicked in and out of the open entrance.

He hissed, "Yes. Oh yes," and arched back to me.

He reached back for my hard cock. I rolled him over then, and he lifted one leg wide and planted the foot high up on one of the bed's corner posts. The other he rested on my shoulder. I could see the dark pools of his eyes in the curtained dimness at the back of the bed and saw that his hands were white knuckled, gripping the carved wood of the back of the day bed frame.

He was still tight, but I worked my cock in a couple of inches and twisted it. He arched his back, opening fractionally, and I was in another inch. Pleased with his hissed cries of strain at taking me, I ran my hand up and down his arched torso, rolling his hard nipples between finger and thumb, rubbing his belly to relax him, then forcing my way in as he cried out, "Yes. Yes."

I took hold of his hips and moved up higher on the bed and moved to the side, not losing my place inside him as I turned him. He had known exactly what to do and now had his legs wide with each foot resting against a corner post as I knelt between his thighs, fucking down into him, watching his face, and playing with his body. He still gripped the back of the day bed with one hand, the other gripping the side of it as he worked his ass back and forth in opposition to my fucking cock. He cried out with pain and pleasure as I rode him, and he vigorously joined the ride.

I came deep inside him, spilling several bursts into his channel, filling him and stroking his heaving belly as if easing the cum deeper into him. He wrapped his legs around me, holding me there, sweat now glistening on both our bodies as our breathing settled.

"So who are you?" he asked again.

"The one you are supposed to be encouraging to buy this place," I replied smiling. As if he didn't already know, I thought.

I was happy feeling his dick filling again under my stroking fingers, and I filled and played his leaking slit with the tip of my little finger.

"I have no idea what you're talking about. You know that? I knew Kyle was trying to sell this place, but there's no reason for me to try to induce you to buy it."

"Sure," I said. "Anyway, what's the deal? Do you come with the house?" I asked, smiling at him, because he was tempting me.

He laughed and began to massage my dick with his ass.

"And if I did? Would that really induce you to buy it?" he asked.

I paused, looking down at him. "You, I want," I said, feeling my cock reloading inside him. "The house? Well there are lots of houses." I had no idea what I wanted except another round with his passage.

"True," he said, "But my house is right on the other side of the river from this one," he added, looking up at me, smiling with lust filed eyes and arching his back and reaching to push my T-shirt off, as I grew inside him.

NIGHT-TIME RENDEZVOUS

"Meet me in the pavilion," Carlo whispered.

"But . . ."

"Wait for me in the pavilion," Carlo whispered again, turning my body away from him, but pulling me into his belly so I could feel his erection pressing up behind me. "See how much I am interested in fucking you?" he added in that deep, husky, amused voice of his.

"Ugh," I grunted, rubbing my butt against his rod, more than ready for the fucking he said he was interested in. "Then why can't I come into the house?" I asked grumpily.

I'd had a two-hour drive getting to the mountainside mansion he was apparently staying at, and now we were standing outside, behind a hedge that ran from the side of the house and along the parking area on the top end of the circular drive. Carlo had been waiting for me and had dragged me behind it as soon as I had arrived.

"My car is just back up the drive," I suggested, "We could fuck in that."

"No. No. The pavilion. I will meet you there, Andrew, as soon as I can," he said persuasively, "Oh, caro mio. Caro mio," he crooned, kissing the back of my neck as I melted and groaned. "You will go through the hedge into . . . onto the side garden, and there you will see the pavilion at the end of the lawn, by the pond. You cannot miss it. But there is a gate in the hedge that runs along that side, and you will have to find that to get through to the lawn," he explained, all the time running his hands around my body, up under my windcheater, and feeling for and squeezing my nipples and pecs.

Then he ran a hand down and cupped my growing dick and tight balls and briefly played with them, murmuring, "Caro mio, oh, you are so beautiful."

"Ohhh, yes," I moaned, reaching back to his butt, "You won't be long?"

"As soon as I can get away," Carlo promised. He released me, I turned, and we fell into a brief kiss before he pushed me away. "You will wait for me in the pavilion—promise," he added, sounding a bit worried.

"Of course," I promised, reassuring him, "But don't be long."

Why we couldn't fuck right then, somewhere closer, I had no idea. But Carlo obviously knew what he wanted, and his dark Latin good looks, hard fitness model's body, and long, thick cock had me under his spell. And that "caro mio" spoken in his husky voice, with its incredibly sexy accent, melted me completely.

He pushed me away, and I headed off in the direction he had pointed me toward. It took me some time to find the gate he had mentioned, and I was getting a bit cold and very fed up with whatever game he was playing by the time I passed through it and onto the lawn on the other side. My enthusiasm wasn't helped by the weather. It had been still and cold, but just as I passed through the gate, snow began to fall.

"Great. Snow," I grumbled and wondered what I was doing there.

But I knew, of course. Carlo, with his black, curly hair, big, dark bedroom eyes, and seductive voice, was irresistible. Add to that a long, thick cock to die for, and a wild abandoned "try anything" love of fucking, and I was his. I knew I was his slave. And so did he. He had been playing with me for a couple of months now, leading me on and then disappearing, keeping me hanging around. I knew he was doing it. But I still couldn't give him up.

We had met at the ski resort of Perisher Blue. I'd tagged along with friends and decided snow wasn't for me, already having decided skiing wasn't for me twenty years before. Carlo was staying in an apartment at Smiggin Holes, but also seemed to be staying at a private lodge.

We'd met in Smiggins Hotel, at the bar. Well, more at the entrance. He had arrived about the same time my friends and I had. Somehow I left with him not long after. We walked to the nearby apartments, and as soon as we were in the door, I was panting and he had his hands—they seemed to be everywhere—and his body, rubbing places that I was moaning for him to keep rubbing and I was groping parts of him I wanted to feel skin to skin.

His cock seemed to magically jump out of his pants and run across my belly as he unzipped me and flipped my package free. His other hand was on my neck, pulling me in for a long, deep kiss. I was usually a top but could go either way, and he was making the moves and I knew he was going to be fucking me. It was a vague thought that was irrelevant. He was in charge, but I was liking it.

Somehow we covered a few meters of floor, and he had pushed me back onto the solid timber coffee table sitting between the two tan suede-covered sofas. And he had stripped my pants, shoes, and socks off as he gracefully settled onto his haunches between my now-spread thighs.

"Mmmm," he hummed. "Caro mio, I am going to fuck you better than you have ever been fucked before," he crooned, with an incredibly sexy Latin accent.

And I believed him. And I wanted him to.

"Prove it," I said huskily.

His mouth closed over the head of my cock, and he sucked and probed into my tiny opening with his tongue, teasing it like an expert. Then his tongue was everywhere, caressing and probing, as his lips tightened and slid, up and down, loosened, and ran around my pole.

"More, yes," I cried, ready to shoot my load and pulling his head in with my hands, my fingers tangling and tugging in his black, glossy curls.

But Carlo backed off instead and in a minute released me. I was begging to come as he held my cock in one hand and began to probe my ass with the fingers of the other. He must have used some lube, but I can't recall when. I just knew when he had a finger up my passage and had landed the tip on my prostate. He wriggled his finger and rubbed till I was moaning, dribbling precum and throbbing and had my legs wrapped around his shoulders. Then finally I came. Carlo's mouth descended onto the head of my cock to catch the cum he was extracting from me as I moaned and writhed.

I was spent as he released my dick and moved up between my legs, and I just looked down at him groggily and in awe, as he began to drive that huge tool of his into my ass. I moaned a lot. And if I didn't know it was going to feel good eventually, I would have yelped and been yelping and flailing about and shouting at him to stop—and meaning it. But instead, I whimpered as he slowly entered me, and I relaxed, willing it to start feeling good. And it did. By the time his thick, black pubic hair was tickling my butt, I was lying there, rolling my head and moaning, "Yes, yes."

The next night we had wound up on a thick white rug on the polished timber floor in front of an open fire in some private lodge. Me on my knees, and him pounding my ass doggy style.

Then he had been gone. But he'd said we could get together again at Coal Point on Lake Macquarie, where he was going to be in a couple of weeks. He'd called me, and I had driven up to the lake from Sydney and found the ochre-colored house on the waterfront, and we had fucked in the horizon lap pool that ran down one side of the patio to end with an unbroken view across the lake. I'd gazed across the water to Belmont for a long time as he fucked me up against the end wall. He'd made sure I left very early the next morning and was grumpily tidying up as I said good-bye. I knew I should say "no" next time he called.

But of course I hadn't. And here I was trudging through the snow. Once I was through the gate and on the lawn I found the pavilion easily, and the fancy Victorian-inspired fantasy of a roof, white with snow, was standing out vividly against the night sky by the time I reached it.

I was relieved to discover that the pavilion's sides weren't open, as I had feared. It was fully enclosed, with narrow French doors opening on several sides of it. The doors I tried first weren't locked, and I entered the building and closed them behind me, glad to be out of the increasing cold. It was dark inside, but I could see the darker shapes of furniture, and as my eyes adjusted to the gloom, I made out what I was sure was a table lamp. I crept carefully over to it and searched for a switch, and was briefly blinded by sudden brightness when I found it. However much I lusted for Carlo, I wasn't going to have waited very long for him in a dark, open, freezing-cold pavilion on a snowy night.

Now that I could see, I found the pavilion was not large but held a comfortable cane sofa, two chairs and a small coffee table piled with magazines. Looking about, I discovered there was an electric heater. I turned that on as soon as I saw it and moved it in front of one of the chairs and sat down, with no idea how long Carlo would take to arrive, but wanting myself and the pavilion both warm when he did.

Then I must have fallen asleep. Because the next thing I knew someone was tapping the top of my thigh, and I was groggily coming too and saying, "Carlo. At last," as I opened my eyes.

But instead of Carlo, I discovered a tall, older man standing in front of me. He was looking down at me, and the light was dim, but I had no trouble seeing the shotgun he held loosely in his hands. It was pointing my way. Its holder had also dropped the barrel so that it was hanging between my spread thighs. It must have been that he had tapped my thigh with it to waken me, I thought, as I sat there very still, stunned, and a bit afraid.

"I'm afraid I'm not Carlo, and I have no idea who you are," he said casually, but not moving.

The temperature was dropping rapidly as the cold air rushed in through an open door, and I shivered. But that cold also brought me out of my shock.

"It's dangerous to point that thing at someone," I said angrily, grabbing the barrel and moving it aside, away from my body. "And you've left the door open."

Unfortunately, there was no way I could get up out of the big deep, chair I was in quickly and neatly with the stranger standing almost between my legs, so I stayed there. For a moment I had thought the man standing in front of me might be a security guard patrolling the grounds, but security guards don't carry shotguns, and they normally wear uniforms with badges. He was in his fifties, but a rugged, muscular fifty with a full head of neat, grizzled hair, a long body, and solid legs. And he was attractive with his tanned skin, full lips, and dark, piercing eyes. Somehow I knew he would laugh easily. He didn't look like a security guard in any way. He was just too polished, too well groomed, and too well spoken. I worried if he was Carlo's current sugar daddy.

My visitor looked momentarily surprised and almost pleased. Then he stepped back to the open door, "I'm sorry. I'm letting out the heat."

Having closed the door, he returned and broke the shotgun open and showed me the breach, "Not loaded," he said, smiling and jiggling the shells in his pocket. "I was going to head out after foxes. They got one of our house cats a few days ago, but then I saw the light in here. I did once break an intruder's arm with it though," he explained, as he opened a tall cupboard I had not noticed, set in the wall between two of the pavilion's doors, and put the shotgun away with two others.

"And who are you?" he asked.

I had no idea what to say or do. I had a vague idea that Carlo lived wherever he found an obliging and generous lover, and I didn't want to spoil his present situation. One reason our affair had been occasional was that I wasn't poor. But I couldn't offer him the sort of lifestyle he obviously enjoyed from the places he had fucked me in. Of course, I had no idea what Carlo's connection to my visitor was.

"My name's Andrew. And it's cold and late and I'd better go," I said, standing up at last and smiling as if I was just some harmless vagrant, and not too bright.

I moved toward the door that the stranger had just closed, but he stepped in front of me.

"You know you are trespassing, don't you?"

"I am trying to leave," I replied. "I'm sorry, I was passing by and it started snowing, so I came in here," I continued, knowing it sounded weak, and he just stood there looking at me, waiting.

"I was asked to come here by a friend," I said eventually, annoyed at the way the man was trying to intimidate me. "Obviously, he's forgotten I'm here, so I'll leave."

The stranger didn't move, and I stepped around him, trying not to show I was still a bit nervous.

"Carlo?" he said. "Tall Latin, with black curly hair, and a body that looks like he should be a male model?" he asked.

I hesitated guiltily, before I replied, "Yes."

"What's he wearing?" he snapped.

"When I saw him he was wearing a pale blue cashmere sweater and washed-out jeans."

"I know him as Hernando," he replied, as he walked over to another cabinet built into a wall of the pavilion. It appeared there was a disguised cupboard built between each of the sets of doors. "Drink?" he asked as he opened this cabinet to reveal a small, but well-stocked bar.

I was caught by politeness, and a bit of curiosity, I confess, so instead of leaving, I said, "A scotch."

"And my name is Grant," the man informed me, stepping over with my drink and then shaking my hand. "And welcome to my pavilion," he added with a smile.

Grant turned on a couple more lamps, and the small pavilion became an oasis of light and warmth, where we sat down opposite each other in the big-cushioned cane chairs and sipped our drinks. Grant was smiling now and looking even better than he had in the dim light. Not usual for a man his age. And I was feeling mildly turned on by him, caused partly by having been ready for Carlo/Hernando, whoever he was, partly by the rush of adrenalin I'd had when I'd first seen Grant with his shotgun, and by the odd situation.

"So have you known Hernando long?" he asked casually.

"I wouldn't say that I know him," I answered equally casually, "We've met a few times, that's all."

"For Hernando, I think that meeting a few times is a pretty serious relationship," Grant responded, smiling widely at his own joke.

I shrugged and decided things were getting complicated and I had better leave when I had finished my drink. I downed the last of it.

"Thanks for the drink," I said, getting up. "Now I had best be off," I added and moved toward the door.

But by the time I reached it, Grant was standing behind me, reaching around me to hold the door handle so I couldn't open the door. His other hand was pressed on my belly, just below my rib cage, pulling me back into his body.

"You're a very sexy man," he was saying, his voice low and husky and his mouth right by my ear. "I can understand why Hernando picked you."

I could feel his warm breath on my neck and smelt the brandy on his breath.

"I want you, Andrew," he told me, his mouth meeting my skin.

I shivered as Grant's lips ran over my neck, giving me little sucking kisses. The hand on my belly stayed there, but his other hand released the doorknob and stroked my rising cock through the fabric of my pants. I'd come out primed for sex. I knew immediately his hand touched my dick that I was going to get it, but just not the way I'd expected.

I grunted my consent as his mouth moved up to my ear.

"I'm a talker, Andrew," Grant said in my ear, his hot breath tickling. "I like to say just what I am going to do when I fuck. Is that OK with you? Are you happy to hear what I'm going to do to your body?"

"Um, I suppose so," I mumbled, not really knowing what he was talking about.

"So, my hand is on your belly, and the other is on your dick. And I am going to run my tongue around inside your ear and see if your cock jumps." He chuckled and I moaned as he swished wetness in my ear, tickling, and, yes, it jumped.

"Hmmm. Nice. Now I think it's time to unzip you and let that nice sausage free, let me see if it looks as good as it feels, and see how nice your balls are. Have you got nice loose balls, Andrew? I like low-hanging balls on a man I'm going to fuck.

"Oh, yes, a nice big meaty piece and—ummmm, heavy balls, full of seed. Do you shoot a big load, Andrew? I bet you do. I can't wait to see the loud you spout for me.

"Hum, do you like that, baby, my thumb on your cap rubbing you while my pinkie is trying to poke into your piss hole? Hmmm, nice and hard, and just a few drops of juice leaking out of you."

I gasped, "Yes, yes," as Grant's hands squeezed my rod and he tugged at my balls. I wanted him to make me come and see how much seed I could shoot for him. Christ. The talk was driving me wilder than his hands and the feel of his thick rod pressing on my lower back were.

"I'm hard, Andrew. You feel that? Feel what you are doing to me? Hmmm. I am going to stir your insides up with my thick piece when I have you nice and open and ready for me. Mmm. Let's get these pants off you and get you naked. How about we both get naked? It's plenty warm enough in here now."

Grant let me turn around then, and as he stripped me off, I unbuttoned and unzipped him and he shed his heavy jacket, a sweater, and his shirt as I pushed his corduroy pants and his briefs down. Gray springy curls spread across his still-muscular chest and surrounded his nipples, then tapered in to run down his belly and into a darker, still-heavy bush. His thick cock was standing out stiffly and heavily veined, and for a few moments we stood belly to belly, and he held our pieces docked and ran his thumb over both heads, slicking the precum about.

"Nice," he said, "But I'm a believer in safe sex, so . . ." He reached for his jacket and his hand emerged with a condom. He passed it to me so I could tear the pack open. "Now roll it on me," he said, his hands massaging my arms now and stroking up from my belly to my chest, playing over my nipples before a hand returned to his jacket for a tube of lube.

"Now that's done, you are going to turn around and I am going to part those cute ass cheeks of yours and take a look at your hole," he said. And I was turning and leaning out along the back of the sofa and spreading my legs for him, panting and reaching for my cock and stroking it, as he continued his sexy monologue.

"Nice butt," he said, "Sweet. I like cheeks I can grab hold of, and yours are big and muscular, and now I have them spread I can see your brown eye winking at me." He chuckled, "You are going to swallow my finger as soon as I get it in you, aren't you, Andrew?"

All I could do was moan, as I felt a thick finger press in past my rim and probe.

"You like getting fucked, I can see, one finger hardly stretches you at all. Nice, so now I'll give you two fingers and stroke up your channel a couple of times and find your prostate with them. Oh yes, that's it, isn't it?" Grant crooned, as I lurched and moaned.

"Yes, yes, there. Fuck," I grunted.

"Mmmm, now three fingers, mm, now we are starting to make your hole open up, aren't we, oh yes. Do you want to come now, Andrew? I want you to come. I want to feel you shoot that load out, and I want to see your cream."

"Fuck me," I gulped. "Fuck me."

"You want to feel my cock inside you? Filling you up, before you come? Stuffing you good? I like that. Because I want to feel my cock in your ass too, Andrew. My cock has been wanting to feel that since I walked in here. You have a beautiful ass, and tight, not too tight, just right. So here comes my cock. Feel it rimming your hole? Mmm, that feels so good, and, oh, baby, I'm going in," Grant moaned.

"I'm in now, Andrew. God, that looks beautiful, my cock sliding in and out of your pucker. Oh, baby, yes, I could work myself in your sweet channel all night. Now come up to me, lift up, here," he reached around and placed a palm on my belly, and I arched back, and up to him.

"Yes. Now kiss me, while I stroke your dick and make you cum," he whispered in my ear.

Our mouths locked and there was a strange, almost silence, for a while, as he fisted my throbbing erection and worked his own cock in shallow strokes inside my channel, until I came. Christ, I spouted cum like there was gallons of it built up, leaning back to him, and he milked it out of me, two, three shots, emptying me as our mouths parted and he began to fuck me deeper and harder, but still holding my belly, and me still arched back. Feeling his cock head rubbing across my spot until he tightened up, "I'm coming. I'm going to fill you with my seed, baby. Oh yes, fuck."

He pumped hard, then jerked and jerked again, and I wished I could feel what he was letting loose flooding me inside. I wanted to feel his cum dribbling out of my ass. Just thinking that had me moan. We hung there for a while, recovering. Then, as Grant's dick slipped out of me, I heard a door open and a draught of cold air blew across me. I turned to see that Carlo, or Hernando, whatever, was standing inside the pavilion and smiling broadly.

"So, he is a good fuck, my friend, Andrew?" Carlo said, moving toward us.

"Your Andrew is a better fuck than you are, Hernando. And I can't wait to see your cock plowing his ass," Grant said, still holding me to him. "Later . . .what do you think Andrew?" he asked me, kissing my cheek, rubbing his face against mine. "Do you want to have my cock buried in your sweet ass, as you fuck Hernando? And later Hernando can fuck you as I plow him," he crooned with his mouth again at my ear, and his hands flying up and down my body as I leaned back against him, reaching for my already-reloading dick as I watched Carlo/Hernando strip off his pale blue cashmere sweater.

NO SURF

"What?"

"No surf today," I repeated, just making idle conversation. "Out there."

Manly beach sat before us under a leaden sky, the low gray clouds moving swiftly, the water a dirty green. A hundred yards out to sea the surfers sat or lay on their boards in a ragged line, rising and falling on the long swell, waiting for waves that seemed unlikely to appear. Occasionally the smooth ocean was spattered and broken by brief showers of rain.

"No. The winds coming off shore and the rain deadens the water," he replied, turning to me fully and appraising me.

I half smiled back, watching his eyes flit up and down me. Then he turned his chair a quarter turn to face me. He was sitting at the small square table next to mine at the Café Steyne.

"You don't look like you're here for the beach," he said, smiling, his eyes indicating my rather overdressed look. Casual but overdressed for a visit to the beach, neat, formal casual, carefully overdressed.

"No," I replied, "No. A doctor's visit."

"Nothing serious?" he asked, making a casual connection.

"No. No. Nothing serious. It's over now. I'm just taking in the view," I offered, feeling the empty place opening up inside me, smiling at him suggestively.

He understood, saying that he lived nearby and was filling in a lazy day.

We entered the apartment, and I moved straight in with little open-lipped kisses. He joined me, my arms going to his neck, his hand to my package, a few squeezes getting me well into him. Then I was pushing against him as we kissed deeper, grinding together as our arms encircled each other and our hands glided over each other.

It's strange how clothes can disappear when you're occupied like that.

I liked the hair on his chest running down his belly. Nice lush black hair on a tanned, worked body. He seemed happy to play his hands over my ass, but I wasn't happy to go that way with him, even feeling what he had for me. Bigger than I could offer him, but it was I who pushed his hand to my engorging piece, suddenly knowing what I needed to fill that empty place that had opened inside me.

I grabbed his hair, pulling his head back, kissing possessively down his neck to his chest. For now, right now, he was mine. And I wanted to feel my flesh throbbing inside him, his body moving under me, writhing before me.

He resisted briefly, knowing he was the fucker, but my mouth and hands, my body, were insistent and he gave in to me. Compromised for me. I felt a rush and turned him, suddenly desperate for the main event. The physical.

He ceased to be; he was nothing and everything. I didn't know him, but my body understood his completely. I pushed him forward on the bed, straddled him and kissed down his spine, wanting to feel each bump of bone, overcome by the perfection of it. Running my fingers over the mounds of hardness before my tongue arrived.

Down to the end where his body separated and split.

I slid back on the bed and pulled his hips up. He lifted his ass to me, making the moves. I was lost now, stroking myself for a moment as I ran my thumb down between his cheeks, over his rim. Then I was in a rush to tongue his entrance, untidy as I lubed him, sighing as my fingers penetrated him and fucked him looser, stroking his smooth passage walls, making him moan and wanting him to moan louder for me.

"Yes," he grunted, as I stroked my fingers again at the same depth.

His arching back had me throbbing and I reached under and held him as I and rolled on a condom and positioned myself and made the first entry, moving in easily, grunting from the overwhelming pleasure of it as he took hold of me deeper and I reached under for his cock and stroked him. I began to move inside him, my hips slipping into the fucking rhythm that was my perfect entry to paradise.

On the edge of my awareness I felt my spine curl and uncurl, smoothly, painlessly, and the empty space inside me started to fill. I rested a hand on his back, low down, feeling his spine moving as my rolling hips guided me in and out of his body.

We lost ourselves separately, me building myself to my climax as he moved his ass in slow circles doing whatever he wanted to take his from me. The empty space inside me was suddenly filled as I grunted and jerked inside him, gripping his hip. My release came, my cream let loose deep inside him as I moaned. I ran my hands over him, under him, took over his cock giving him the final few strokes he needed to come. Catching his cream in my hand, wiping it on his belly.

I fell away and pulled him in to me, feeling his warmth, his firmness.

"You've got a beautiful back," I said, running my fingers lightly along his spine.

"Are you into backs?"

"No. Yes," I replied, confused, "Right now I just appreciate how amazing they are. I had a problem."

"You seemed fine to me," he said, turning his head so I could kiss his mouth.

"Yes. It's gone, all gone. I found out today."

"Oh. So this is a celebration fuck," he said, and laughed, rolling around so he faced me, his hand moving to my right nipple, his mouth to my neck.

"Yes," I said smiling at him, not in a hurry to go anywhere else, "Yes. A celebration."

SURRENDER

The train ride was smooth. The carriage seeming to glide along almost soundlessly. "This is a smooth ride," he said, "Like going up in a hot air balloon. Have you done that?"

Matt grunted, glancing up from his laptop's screen, hand's poised, flickering fingers momentarily stilled before he looked back.

Outside the train window the gray day and dusky green and brown of the bush flowed past, seemingly endless.

"So?" he asked.

"Umm," was Matt's only answer, and a hand briefly touching his knee. Reassuring physical contact.

They passed a shallow lagoon where clumps of thin grass-like reeds were standing erect in the water, reminding him of islands. Some congregated into large masses, others alone, small outposts in the still, gray water.

"So, what did you think?" he persisted.

Matt looked up, a touch annoyed at being dragged away from his work.

"It's small. Nice location, but hardly room to turn around. You know I like space and comfort."

Matt returned to his work, and his lover looked out of the window again. Something catching in his throat for a moment and swallowed. He liked cool days, days like today, not hot, not cold, cool. Everything. It was the first and last time Matt went to his house.

At first he'd thought that Matt was playing with him, had little need of him. He'd suggested things they could do together and Matt would say they were on his list, but never seemed to get around to that part of his list.

Then they would meet and he made Matt arch, writhe, moan, and sigh as he made love to his still nearly perfect body. Until it was Matt's turn to devour him. In those moments Matt would be there as he never was otherwise, exploring him, making love to him. But saying occasionally, as a casual observation, things like, "It's a shame you're so small," stroking and sucking his small cock as Matt's own filled again to its full eight inches.

So there were other men, and in the first heat, he'd shared Matt, giving it little thought. Sucking him while some muscular, well-hung man plowed Matt's ass to appreciative moans, and gasps of, "Yes, more, god, that's good. Turn, yes. Like that. Oh yes." And he wondered why he seemed to remain while the well-hung golden-bodied men moved on in a slowly passing parade.

Matt did little to build anything between them. It was he who'd needed the daily contact and established the phone calls as a pattern. Then he discovered one day that Matt had become accustomed to them like some mildly addictive drug.

He had been surprised and suddenly overcome by the discovery that he really was wanted. And he'd wondered what Matt wanted, making a great effort to discover it. But with no change in Matt's manner to him, he gave up. In the end he realized that he would get what Matt gave him and could only easily give what it was natural for him himself to give.

They lay in bed one day and Matt said, "I'm getting a bigger apartment. There'll be enough room for both of us."

Matt said it looking into his eyes, but matter-of-factly. A statement, not an invitation.

He'd said nothing, not sure if Matt was actually asking him to move in, and stunned to blankness by the remark.

Matt had moved and soon after he'd asked petulantly, "When are you moving in?" A forgone conclusion. Now he was being slow and inconsiderate not being there.

"I wasn't sure you were serious," he'd replied, confused, pleased, lost.

He'd thought of one thing, though. The only time he'd been there at night they had spent the night together, Matt cupped into his lap.

"We sleep together," he'd said.

"There are two bedrooms," Matt replied, frowning.

"If I move in, we sleep in the same bed."

Matt shrugged.

He moved in, keeping his clothes in the other bedroom. Matt's own wardrobe was extensive, with his clothes overflowing into the second bedroom, but Matt had cleared a couple of drawers in the chest for him and complained when he didn't use them. So he moved his underwear in there, into the chest in their bedroom.

The well-hung bronzed gods continued to pass through, leaving their impression briefly in Matt's stretched and well-stroked ass, but rarely returning.

One day he came home to find one of them there again, plowing Matt as they kissed deeply. He'd gone cold seeing them. Suddenly terrified that it was over, that something he'd never known for sure he'd had was gone.

But Matt had turned his sex-drugged face and signaled him over, pulling him to him and taking his mouth, moving a hand inside his pants, moaning as the bronzed god continued to plow him.

Then the bronzed god left and Matt plowed him as if he never wanted to stop, the sky beyond the glass wall turning dark until a golden moon and a million stars hung in it like Christmas ornaments. And at some time when his lover was resting inside him, subsiding from the last fuck, Matt had whispered in his ear, "I love you."

It was almost as if Matt's words had escaped during a lapse in concentration and they rolled about, occupying his mind, until they turned into a phrase he had read once "Life isn't coherent, and it doesn't fit into neat boxes."

And he wondered if he had the courage to truly surrender himself to it.

TEMPLE VIRGIN

I had been minding my own business and preparing the temple for the first festival of spring, the ancient celebration of the planting of the first seed. Going out into the nearby hills in search of branches of buds and the first leaves and small flowers to adorn the alter was tiring work, but it needed to be done. As the offerings I found would last only a day or so, my first collecting could only be done the day before the festival began. As was the ancient custom, I did my collecting naked, and I piled the scratchy twigs and other gatherings into a small cart pulled by Nanny, the goat.

On my way out at first light I followed the new road the Romans had laid, going for a mile or so along it before making my way into the hills, and in the evenings I usually returned the same way.

On this morning it was chilly, and I shivered as I left just before sunrise, eager for the day to heat up.

I had gone a mile or so and decided it was time to strike off into the hills. I left the road along a clear track and lost myself in looking about for the first signs of a fertile spring and saw none.

"Friend," I heard a voice call.

I hesitated and looked about but could see nothing.

"Here, friend, help me," the strong deep voice called again.

I was sure that I now knew where the voice had come from, and leaving Nanny and my cart, went to investigate. At the bottom of a small gully I found a giant barbarian smiling up at me. The last winter rain had made the sides of the gully slippery and I could clearly see where the man had tried to get out, but had slipped back in. He was coated in mud now, and, looking up and down the gully, I saw he was possibly trapped in there. It was mud all about, and the small trees had been knocked down by a mudslide at one end. It seemed that he was now effectively in a pit.

"I am not strong enough to pull you out," I said to him, seeing his predicament. "But I can look for some branches that may help you."

"Thank you," he said, smiling at me.

He was a man of huge proportions, and I wondered at the size of the only part of him that was hidden, that which lay beneath a large loincloth. But I stopped myself wondering, because I was a virgin bound to the temple till the end of the new spring, only able to leave when the grain had grown tall and set its seed. Yes, I thought with longing, I was now of age and in a few more months I would be freed of my vows. I was finding I was no longer satisfied by only giving my seed to the gods. And tomorrow spring was here and. Ah, well. Then . . . Ah, then. My organ stirred as it always did when I had such thoughts.

I wandered back and found some large pieces of fallen wood and lowered them in to him so that he soon had a sort of path a couple of feet up the mud slide. He walked right back and ran up to it and in a few strides was out and over the top. It had seemed to be easy for him, and I wondered he hadn't been able to do that earlier. He was obviously extremely strong and fast, his huge mud-covered muscles not just for show.

He came up to me. "Ah, my fine young friend," he said, "I should reward you."

"No, that is not necessary," I replied, "and I must be off as I have much to do collecting greenery for the temple for the festival tomorrow."

"You gather offerings for fertility?" he said, looking me over. "Then I shall reward you as a man is best rewarded in spring," he said, and picked me up and lowered me into the gully.

I was dumbfounded and more so as he jumped in beside me. Then he lifted some litter from the floor of the gully to reveal dry soil and a pile of belongings, including a fine fur cape, which he spread on the ground. Then he grabbed me by the waist and lifted me so that my manhood was at his mouth. He was amazingly strong. He sucked me into his huge mouth, and I flailed at him, wanting to escape, because I was a virgin bound to the temple. A virgin to women and men both. Young men such as I served the temple gods until we were in our prime. Then we married well. But till then we served only the temple gods.

But my manhood did not obey my wishes. It grew rapidly in the barbarian's mouth as he held me high. I heard a moan and knew it was me, as my hands grasped his hair and twisted it about. When he lowered me he pushed my face to his own huge weapon. I had not seen it earlier, because a mud-dripping loincloth, now gone, had covered it. The weapon I saw before me was huge, thick, long, and of a deep, strong color. In fear, I opened my mouth, and he pushed his huge cock head between my lips.

"Suck," he ordered, shaking my head to rattle some sense into it, for my manhood was throbbing and I was confused. Then I did as he said, sucking and licking him until he pulled free.

"Good," he grunted.

I ached for my own release now, and he pushed me back onto the fur rug and fell to his knees between my thighs, pushing them wide. He then fell on my manhood and sucked me to emptiness in moments, his huge mouth swallowing and vibrating against my whole length, making me cry out he pulled the seed from me so fiercely.

When he released me, I lay back gasping, but I cried out again almost immediately as he lifted my backside in his huge hands and set my hole to his mouth. I scrabbled about, resting back on my shoulders and looking up my belly in shock, to the great lion-like head moving between my thighs.

He flipped my legs back then and I gasped as I could now see his mouth at that brown-rimmed hole of mine that no one but me had ever touched since my own mother had last wiped it clean.

I gaped, open mouthed, horrified he would want to lick that place, then whimpered and writhed in pleasure with the feel of what this strong thick tongue was doing to me there.

Then he lowered me. I cried out and tried to escape. I was most confused and afraid at this time, for he had lowered my now-soggy, twitching hole to his hips and supporting me with one arm about my belly was guiding his huge weapon to me.

"No. No. I am a temple virgin," I cried out, again, and again, as he tried to push the head of his huge cock into me. "No. You must not enter me," I cried. And in truth I said "must" as part of me had been longing to know the feel of a man's weapon entering me and possessing my passage powerfully.

"No. No. What are you doing?" I cried again, knowing full well what he intended.

He ignored, me and, in a searing burst of pain, had stretched me so my hole allowed that huge bulbous cap to enter it. I opened my legs automatically as he moved his weapon about inside me and slowly the pain lessened, then he wasted little time in burying the rest of himself in me to the accompaniment of my cries and struggles.

Oddly, though, I began to feel a strange pleasure from being filled so fully, and when he began to move his buried weapon inside me, I groaned and bucked, more with a taste for the movement than with pain.

Soon I was yelling in wonder and humping up and thumping my hips to his as he plowed his weapon in and out of me, and he grunted and laughed as he worked every part of my passage, until he threw his head back and roared. I knew what was flooding into me then was his seed, and it gushed free inside me as I moaned with pleasure, but also confusion, knowing that he had taken my virginity and filled me with his seed on the day before the festival began.

When he finally released me, he tossed me up to the top of the gully like a stuffed doll, and he lay back on his fur rug.

"Um, but you are trapped again," I said hesitantly, looking down at him.

"No. I can get out of here any time I want to," he replied, closing his eyes to sleep.

I was even more confused and weak kneed and smiling foolishly as I left him, and I could feel his seed leaking from my hole and running down my thighs. But then I realized that I was undone. "I am no longer a virgin." I cried. "My part in the festival will be a lie. Woe to my people. The gods will punish us, will punish me; and the priests will punish me," I cried in anguish.

"None shall know," the barbarian said, "and you shall still be a virgin to the Gods, I shall intercede with them if you remain silent about what has passed. I am favored by them. Which is how I knew you would pass this way. Now go, so I may converse with the Gods in private, and remember, silence."

"Oh, you can do that? Talk to the God's?"

"Yes. None shall know what passed here if you do not tell them. Be gone now, before I change my mind."

I hurried away afraid to anger him and trembling with relief that he was such a powerful barbarian. Nanny and my cart were fortunately waiting only yards away as I was walking oddly and in a daze. I had to believe the barbarian. If I had displeased the Gods the festival would be a failure and my people's crops would wither in the fields. Once I moved off though I found my offerings immediately, where I was sure none had been before. They were now everywhere and my heart filled with joy to know the Gods were pleased with me, and it was obviously going to be a very fertile year.

THE ACTING LESSON

It was supposed to be a party of some sort. There was a lot of money involved and I liked money, particularly lots of it. And the guy who had rung, Greg, was an old client. I hadn't seen him for about six months, true, but he had been a regular for about a year before that. Often one on one, but just as often two or three plus me. And occasionally a party, which had always involved two or three escorts, plus the client's guests. He had always paid well and without any argument. And I had charged big for the party nights. Sometimes his guests liked to get a bit rough.

I worked out and knew how to look after myself, though, without having to use any muscles except the ones they paid me to use. So I didn't hesitate to say yes when Greg called.

It was the usual big Toorak mansion screened from the street by a hundred-year-old hedge. I gave my name at the gates and got let in and headed up the cream gravel drive to where a guard with a Doberman, on a very short leash, showed me where to park my car.

"Nice," I said as I got out, looking up at the glowing windows with their swag curtains.

153

The guard gave me a cold stare, colder even than his Doberman's, but he led me to the front door and grunted something into a camera. I wondered if I should have charged Greg more and what add-ons I could put on his tab. He'd said only four or five friends. If it was more I'd add extra for each of them, I decided, and he'd said rough, but nothing I hadn't done before. I wasn't sure what I had done before, but hey, I was sure I'd notice if I did something new, and I'd add it on.

I was let in by a rather hot young guy, a genuine blond for sure. I could see all his body hair as he stood before me and also that he was excited about the event.

"It looks as if the party has started without me," I said.

He just turned and walked down the wide hallway.

"Great," I muttered, watching his bulbous butt rolling enticingly. The other talent thought he was a star.

Blondie opened half a double door, made of dark polished timber, and I went in right behind him. Greg immediately pulled me aside and into a deep kiss. He was a big kisser and had a hand on my assets, massaging them. I happily fell into a bit of foreplay, enjoying the kiss and running my hands exploringly over him. When we pulled apart, I saw we were in a large formal dining room. But very dimly lit. And entrée was a bit unusual. The blond was lying across the very end of the polished mahogany table being enjoyed by two guests. One sitting down comfortably as he was sucking the blond's cock, pulling at his balls, and probably doing other things, as he seemed to have no spare hands. A double snack I thought observing the second guest who was standing, feeding his cock in a very energetic way in and out of the blond's throat, his head hanging back over the edge of the table.

A couple of other men were sitting at the table watching. Both had their hands busy with their tools. Greg led me over to them with a hand on my ass. We stopped in

154

front of a jowly solid man, middle aged but hard, in all ways. Greg stood behind me, cupping my pecs through my T-shirt, as the guy reached over and unzipped me and slid my jeans down to reveal the package. He had a good feel, as if not sure he wanted to buy, then he grunted and Greg turned me about, and I got the message and bent over. Jowly obviously considered his purchases carefully before he took delivery. He also felt the width and internal quality. His fingers were thick, and I wriggled my ass on them, smiling as he added another and grabbed my filling cock between my legs with the other hand and began to tug at it. I had my face level with Greg's fly, and not wanting to see him left out, unzipped him.

But Jowly had other ideas. "He can wait," he grunted, slapping my ass and pulling me about.

His eyes were hooded now as he stroked me up. His companion continued stroking himself, moving his eyes from Jowly's hands working my cock and balls to the double feeding happening just feet away at the end of the table. The blond came and the guy at his butt stood up as Blondie[using as a name substitute] spread his legs. In a moment Blondie was being fucked at both ends. But no one was in a rush, it was slow fucking as the two guys began to do some hand work on Blondie and each other. Blondie arched and writhed, giving them both a good time. But they were being pretty brutal with their hands too by the look of it, and I didn't think all the writhing was put on.

Jowly had me pretty big by now, and I looked down at him. He still looked undecided. This wasn't the usual sort of party I had done for Greg. He'd been in charge before, and the crowd had been happy, horny, and glad of a fuck session. These guys looked hungry, mean, and not happy. I had a first small twinge of doubt about the session.

"He'll do," Jowly suddenly said, grunting.

A lot of tension suddenly seemed to go out of the air. Behind me, I felt Greg relax. It was obvious whose party it was and I was a bit annoyed. I didn't know Jowly from the proverbial. And Greg's nervousness had me suddenly thinking the Doberman might make it as hard for me to leave the mansion as it would be for anyone unwanted to get in.

Greg started licking and fingering my ass as Jowly had me bend over and start to service him. He was a good size and growing nicely when I vaguely sensed someone else moving behind me. Greg moved and suddenly my ass was being shared, the fingers stroking and fucking me so strongly I gulped on Jowly's big dick, as I used a hand on his balls and inner thighs.

I was still dressed and someone pulled my jeans back up my thighs so only my butt was naked. Jowly grunted as I felt a thin cock slide into me. I was fucked by that for a while as Jowly grunted and hardened. He had a good view of whoever was plowing my ass and after a few minutes leaned forward over me and I felt him playing behind me too, him obviously getting off on feeling the other guys cock as it drove in and out. My head was buried in Jowly's lap, and I did my best to keep up my own bobbing action as I got crushed there and Jowly got more interested in the action at my rear.

My jeans dropped to my knees, and a hand had slipped between my thighs and was tugging at my cock, I had no idea whose, and I didn't care. I was having trouble breathing, with my mouth full, and my nose crushed in Jowly's pubes. My face was buried in his pants.

The cock in my ass was replaced. A bigger, thicker one now, and bent. Providing a driving bent action that had me twitching and losing concentration, glad the hand had gone from my dick, because I was having enough trouble concentrating on Jowly already. He was grunting more and had both hands at my ass now, spreading my cheeks then poking a finger in with the cock, stretching me, exploring me deeply, so that the cock's owner changed his action, going to short, shallow rapid pumps.

Then Jowly was grunting again and stroking my ass cheeks, moaning, "Beautiful. Oh, yes, beautiful."

He was hard but not giving any sign of being ready to come yet. Even though I was doing the best job I could in my crushed cramped position, and my best was very good, I knew.

The cock left my ass, and Jowly growled as he sank several fingers of both hands inside my hole and pulled. I bucked and gulped at his roughness as he tugged me open and probed. I was leaking and hard and being ignored, and short of breath. Then Jowly grunted loudly and a cock was trying to make its way inside me before Jowly removed anything. I tried to say something but discovered that I was stuck where I was, someone had tied my hands to something behind Jowly's back, and I couldn't even pull my head back to get some relief from his thick rod as it filled my throat, I was now genuinely uncertain.

As the new cock made its way in, Jowly grunted and pulled at my asshole. I was in pain. And the way he was trying to rip me open was never going to turn to pleasure. The cock was fortunately quite thin once the head was in, and I took it and Jowly's thick fingers with difficulty, but I did it. I increased my sucking and tongue work as best I could, squashed and having difficulty breathing, wishing Jowly would come so I could breathe again.

I felt the guy inside me cum and then slip out, and Jowly grunted his approval and tried to get his fingers in deeper, then gave up and was pulling my cheeks apart again. I was doing everything I could with my experienced mouth, but Jowly seemed no closer to coming than he had been when the first cock occupied my passage.

The fourth cock was there now and I had a feeling Jowly was guiding it in, his hand seemed to have stopped tugging and probing me. But it was only a temporary relief.

Once that cock was inside he wanted to share with it. Unfortunately this was a big one, and if Jowly hadn't been inconsiderate and determined, and I hadn't been immobilized, he would never have got as many of his fingers inside me as he did. I was having trouble doing anything with the cock in my mouth, as I was now genuinely short of breath and gagging with pain. And the cock in my rear was hard and powerful. Its owner's hips pounded my ass brutally as Jowly pulled and probed at me.

All Jowly's cock was doing was suffocating me. I began to choke around it as my legs were pulled wider, and Jowly leaned even further over me, improving his view of my tortured ass. The way he had me he was cutting off my air supply almost completely. I began to panic. Hands went to my cock and balls as I started to kick my legs about wildly, jerking myself back trying to get my face out of his groin and air into my nose, my mouth choked with cock, my nose never good for breathing at any time squashed into his groin. Jowly grunted and seemed to crush my head more as my mouth tried to gape around his thick piece, forced down my throat.

I was getting dizzy and had gone past panic to mindless terror. Suddenly, I was feeling weak and aware of myself coming in burst after burst after burst, the pleasure of ejaculating overcoming me, leaving me ready to pass out. The guy fucking me bottomed hard and came as Jowly's fingers withdrew. And my legs folded up.

And at that moment Jowly filled my mouth with cum, giving a huge shudder that momentarily released the pressure on my face as he unbent to arch back. I gasped, choking on cum and saliva as he came again, and I breathed a rasping suck of air through my nose, now no longer bent and crushed into his pubes.

More cum flooded my throat but I got air in too at last, my head spinning as my hands were freed suddenly and I fell onto the floor, my chest heaving as I gasped desperately for air, cum dribbling from my mouth and being splattered on my face as Jowly came again all over me. It had taken him a damn long time to come, but now he had started he didn't seem to want to stop. I lay there gasping, finally opening my eyes after a few minutes to look up and see Jowly smiling as Greg huddled over him licking his cock clean.

As I got my breath back, I felt myself begin to shake. I was in shock and I felt as if I had been fucked all night. I was exhausted and sore and aching. I struggled up but Jowly put a huge foot on my chest and pushed me back down. I was still too shaky to fight him, knowing I would need to be fully recovered before I even tried.

Jowly said, "Greg will show you out when he's finished cleaning me up."

I almost cried with relief and looked around to see the blond was pouring drinks and only one other man remained in the room with us. He watched blankly, tugging absently at his soft cock, flopped in his lap, as I lay gasping on the floor with my jeans around my knees, and Greg finished licking Jowly clean.

When he was done, Greg showed me out into the passage, immediately shoving an envelope into my hand.

"He's given you double what we agreed," Greg said, smiling, and I automatically flicked through the notes, seeing he was right. "Very good job you did. Very realistic the way you pretended to struggle and panic. The gasping was great. Great acting. Just what he likes. He wants you back next Tuesday night, 8:00 PM again."

THE QUAINT VILLAGE INN

The small pub I entered looked friendly. The bar was open, with a low, oak-beamed ceiling blackened by centuries of smoke from the fire burning in the open hearth to one side, by pipe smoke, and, in recent, years by the smoke of cigarettes.

The voices of its occupants made a pleasant background hum in the comfortable room, and as there was a small table vacant away from the fire, I sat down at it. The barman had been cheerful and fast. "It's only the best beer you'll have here, sir," he had assured me. "Made right there in the village."

It was certainly a good beer and also a good sales pitch. I knew it couldn't be true, because all beer was made in big breweries nowadays, not quaint villages.

"Yes sir, we have a room," the same barman had assured me when I had first arrived and a young woman had been called in through a door behind the bar and cheerfully shown me up to a small but comfortable room furnished with what looked like genuine ancient furniture as old as the pub building itself appeared to be. For a moment

I felt I had stepped back in time. But the woman's clothes didn't support that view. There was a peasant look to her outfit, but it was definitely modern.

"Anything you want, sir, just ask. Breakfast is from 7:00 to 8:00 AM in the dining room. We do a traditional breakfast. Hot and filling. We aim to please, sir," she added with a saucy smile. If I had been interested in a pretty young woman, I wondered how far her aim to please might have gone.

I found an old-fashioned bathroom down the corridor and freshened up before I went back down the narrow stairs and reentered the bar. "Very nice," I thought. A very nice and unexpected surprise to find such an historic and friendly place. I would have to note it down and let my friends know about it. The small forest I had driven through just before arriving also promised some unspoiled walking trails. And the village itself, well, it looked like a postcard, and I wondered what TV shows or movies had been filmed there. It was too perfect not to have made it onto the screen at some stage.

I had not long been seated when a very smart-looking young man in a loose shirt and baggy pants separated himself from a group at the bar and moved toward me. "Mind if I join you, sir?" he asked with a broad smile.

"Yes, of course, please do join me," I said, indicating the three empty seats at the small table. He introduced himself as Josh.

"And what has brought you to our small village then, sir? We get very few visitors; it's not easy to find."

"Chance, Josh," I replied, with a smile, more than pleased to talk to such a good-looking young man. "Pure chance. I have no idea how I got here, really. I am just taking any interesting-looking road or turning and seeing where it leads me, but I do have to arrive at Holleystone

Grange by the end of the week. And this quaint village pub is where the twists and turns of today's drive have led me."

He gave a small chuckle. "Ah, chance is an amazing thing, sir, isn't it?" His eyes twinkled, and there was some other look there that made my knees feel weak, though I was getting hard elsewhere. I hadn't had any for a couple of weeks.

"Yes. Yes, chance is an amazing thing, but I must make a note of how to get here, as this is the sort of place I'd like to come back to. What is the nearest town?" I asked him.

"I'll have to think on that, sir. There are several nearby."

I might have thought it was an odd answer if I had not been so taken by him, but I was taken, and I didn't give it much thought.

"If you really want to come back, I am sure you will find the way, sir," he added, and his face took on a look of satisfaction.

I had vaguely been aware of the door to the bar opening and glanced up to see someone entering, an older man, very smartly dressed, and with a serious look on his face. I'd have given him no more than that brief glance if he had not fixed his eyes on me and turned toward our table. My companion looked up at him. "Good evening, sir," he said and the new arrival made a small movement with his hand.

"I'd best leave you, sir," Josh said, standing up and winking at me. I was going to protest he should stay when the older man said, "May I?" and took Josh's place.

He seemed to be examining me in a very personal way that made me feel naked. It was a possessive look. A dominating look and a lustful look all at once. If I had been firming up to Josh, I was unexpectedly getting even more aroused by the new arrival. "Robert," he said with a big smile, "I think we need to get to know each other better."

I had no idea what to respond. And no words came to me until he had moved his chair beside mine and, placing an arm about my shoulders, moved his face to mine for a kiss. "No," I blurted out, as I pulled back in surprise and worry and looked about. But the small crowd in the bar seemed not to care. They were not oblivious to us, though, as I saw Josh smiling at me, or at us, and then stepping over. He bent over me and whispered, "Just relax for his lordship."

I was stunned. This was a quaint old country pub bar we were in, not some gay club in Soho. And the days of the local lord taking who he pleased, whenever he pleased, were long gone. Josh stood back and returned to sipping his beer, watching us with a hooded smile. Meanwhile, his lordship had a hand unzipping my jeans as his mouth found mine and I allowed him a tentative kiss. The background hum in the bar was unchanged, as if this was normal. And perhaps it was, my confused brain decided, as now his lordship had my jeans opened out and my briefs pushed down and his free hand wrapped about my stiffening cock. Josh seemed to have moved around for a better view, and I felt a shot of arousal hit me. Oddly, I felt safe, but I also felt there was no way for me to escape from whatever was about to happen to me, because Josh now had a firm hold of both my wrists.

His lordship pulled my face to his for another kiss, and I let him possess my mouth as I spread my legs and hooked one over the arm of my chair to help my balls be pulled up free of my briefs and allowed fingers to tug them and then move down to seek my entrance.

When I came up for air. Josh was kissing his lordship's clothes off him, that was what it looked like, his head moving all over the muscular and hairy body being revealed as the expensive clothes he wore were pushed aside by Josh's searching mouth. His lordship smiled at me and stroked me up and down with one hand as his other hand slowly removed my clothing. I dreamily glanced at the bar and saw that the men there were now smiling at me, and while they still talked among themselves, they were also obviously enjoying the action at my table. A burly farmer walked over and bodily moved my chair around so I faced his lordship and he was given a smile for his troubles. "Anything to oblige you, sir," he said with a lewd chuckle. Then he pushed me forward so my T-shirt could be fully removed and lifted me up under the arms so his lordship could pull my jeans off me. Then he bent over and removed my shoes and socks while one of his hands strayed to cup and squeeze my balls.

"Test him, Roly," his lordship purred and the farmer smiled broadly and waggled great thick fingers at me before he moved them between my thighs and beneath my sac to find my hole. I gasped and moaned and gasped some more as he tested me well with those thick fingers, then while his lordship stroked and Roly probed deeper, I came in a great jerk and spouting, between the three of us.

"Hmmmmm," Roly murmured,

"Hmmmmmm, very nice," his lordship added. "A fine gift for our special day."

"Hmmmmm, a fine spouting," Josh added, bending and kissing me.

I sat there, my legs spread and raised over my chair's arms, naked and spent, but aware that the three men were smiling and licking their lips.

"Move him for me, Roly," his lordship ordered, and Roly grabbed me under the arms and Josh took hold of my legs and they lifted me and carried me over to the low bar.

I had wondered at the height of the bar when I had arrived. I had assumed it was because our ancestors were so much shorter than we are, but even so, waist high seemed low. But when they laid me on it, I knew it was just the right height and width for what his lordship was looking forward to that night.

"We have had a fine one step into this pub for our pleasure tonight, lads," he said. "So, another drink all round as I show you what this prize young man is made of."

There was a low cheer as drinks were ordered all around, with the barman passing them over the bar either side of me as his lordship lifted my legs, handing one to Josh and one to Roly, as he moved between them and I finally saw what he had growing up between his legs. I tried to pull away. "Shhh, shh," Josh murmured, "You'll love it," Roly boomed with a laugh. "I've tested you, remember."

I wailed as his lordship entered me in a burst of pain before he had slid in to the point of generating some pleasure, and stopped, allowing me to adjust. My further cries were stopped by the barman taking hold of my head and pulling it back so it hung over the side of the bar and letting his own hard organ flop against my open lips. I opened them wider to cry out my objections to the pain when the barman pressed between my lips and I was too busy sucking and gagging on him to make any more objections to what his lordship was doing at a lower orifice. And then to what someone was doing to that other tiny orifice. I was lost. The dick in my ass was now doing magic things inside me, possessing me completely and working me up to another spouting as something explored the opening in my cock head. I jerked and came as the barman pulled from my mouth and spouted over my chest. There was a cheer from the other men in the bar, and then I felt a great flood inside me as his lordship jerked and came. Another small cheer went up, and husky voices asked who was next, and I heard grunts and moans, as he pulled free. I felt Josh's hands swapped for another pair and felt someone else move between my thighs and tried to rise up to see what was going on, very much wanting to see what was going on as the small pub crowd made a toy of me.

"Let him look," someone cried out and my head was pushed up and something was wedged beneath me as I

165

goggled at what I saw. Josh was there between my legs, a big smile on his face as he waggled a huge throbbing cock at me, and beyond him all the men in the bar were naked and all were presentable and all were hard and erect and looking at me with lascivious eyes. I moaned and whimpered.

"Robert, Robert," his lordship crooned, leaning into me and kissing me, "you will remember this night for years to come, as will we. It's rare we get such a fine, virile visitor on this night."

"Aye, you will," Josh murmured as he worked his organ into me. I am sure I came again, perhaps several times, but soon it was a blur of men between my thighs and mouths on my cock and balls and men moving their manhood between my lips.

I woke in the ancient bed in the small, quaint bedroom upstairs, naked and covered in cum, to find his lordship there, also naked and working himself up for me. He striped back the sheets, exposing my exhausted body.

"I can't resist one last time," he said, climbing into the bed, spreading my legs, and impaling me on his great dick, my hole so wet and well stretched he slid straight in. When he was done, he left the room and I dozed fitfully, then became aware of the time and of the need to be on the road.

I arrived downstairs with my overnight bag, almost falling down the stairs my legs were so weak and I was so sore.

"Ah, at last. We kept breakfast warm for you," the young woman who had shown me to my room the previous day said cheerfully as I reached the last step. She ushered me into a small dining room set for one and dashed off to return with a plate overflowing with poached eggs and bacon, sausages and toast, and tomatoes and mushrooms. "I won't be able . . ." I said, looking at it in alarm.

"Oh my, after the night they gave you," she said with a laugh, "I am sure you will manage to eat it all. I will bring you a nice pot of tea to wash it down and rehydrate you. I doubt there is anything left in you, poor man."

Her cheerful concern was disconcerting, and I started on the food cautiously, but I have to admit I did eat almost all of it before I stood up.

"Who do I pay the bill to . . . for the room and breakfast?"

"Oh," she laughed, "no charge to you, sir. His lordship was well pleased with what you provided him. Oh, no charge at all. And, see, you did eat it. You will need your strength, you know. But you had best be on the road, or you won't get to where you are going this year," she added, suddenly seeming sad. "Yes, you had best go now," and she was handing me my overnight bag and leading me to the door out of the pub and out to my car. She seemed to want to hurry me off. "Go straight ahead on this road, sir. Don't turn off the road till you are through the forest and reach the next town. Then it's safe to stop. They have a good pub there, sir, I have heard. They do a very fine lunch, so I have heard."

I drove off in a daze, exhausted, aching, sore, and confused. She waved to me and was still waving when I rounded a corner that hid her from view. I passed through the forest that seemed to surround the village and followed the road straight on. To be honest I was too tired to even think of turning off and exploring today. And within an hour I was entering Aberanthruwth. I stopped, thirsty and tired and thinking I might even take a room there for the night. I went into the bar and the smell of fresh coffee greeted me. I ordered a cup and a sandwich.

"Where have you come from today, sir?" the waitress asked politely.

"Oh, the village up the road, in the forest," I admitted nervously.

"The village, sir? And which one was that then?" she asked conversationally.

"Um, I don't know its name. Very pretty, like a postcard. All oak beams and white plaster and stone and a . . . pub, a very quaint pub. Perhaps you can tell me what the village is called."

She looked at me oddly. "And this pub, sir, did you stay there the night?"

"Yes," I said, feeling sure I was blushing. "Yes I did. Very . . . comfortable."

"And the room, sir, what was it like?"

I wondered where this was heading. "Um nice, the bed and the furniture seemed very old."

"As old as the inn, sir?" she asked quietly.

"Um yes," I replied, looking for some clue as to what she was asking all this for.

"And was it a woman or a man who took you up to your room, sir,"

"A woman. Why? Is there something l . . . ?"

"Ah," she said with a sigh, suddenly looking crestfallen, "Then I will be of no interest to you, sir. You'd have seen this lordship then. If you stay the night here, Norman will be more to your taste then."

"What is this all about?" I asked her angrily, tired of games.

"Why the village, sir. It can only be reached once a year, and if you like men in your bed, then it's a woman shows you your room and it's his lordship who greets you . . . as you know. But if you like women, then a young man shows you to your room, and then it's her ladyship who has you for the night."

"But that sounds like some legend," I said with a laugh, wondering what sort of strange woman I had come across.

"Oh yes, sir, its the legend. But it's true, isn't it? I have heard of it, but you are the first one I have met who

168

has been there. So, do you want a room for the night, sir?" she asked eagerly. "It's only the most virile they let stay the night. Their staying power is legendary, so they say, sir."

A great hulking brute in rough work clothes had entered the room and was looking at me now. "This is Norman. I know Norman will be ready for you," She added, looking at me in a very disturbing way.

"No. No, I have to be somewhere tonight. Friends, they are expecting me. Sorry," I said and hurried my coffee down and left, eager to put as much distance as possible between myself and my previous nights lodging as I could, but taking careful note of the date.

TOUCHING TIME

I woke to the touch of a hand stroking up my thigh. It rested briefly on my hipbone, but I was suddenly more concerned by what I felt at my wrists. I was tied there with something soft, but firmly tied, unable to pull my arms down from where they were above my head. I panicked for a moment. My eyes were covered. I was blindfolded. My heart took a jump and skipped in rapid beats as the hand at my hipbone moved upward. Another hand touched my shoulder and began to slip across my collarbone. I gasped and twisted at the feel of them.

"Who's there?" I whispered fearfully, "Whose hands are they?" I got no answer and heard only the sound of soft music in the background. "Who are you?" I cried out quietly.

Then another hand, larger, wider, landed gently on my belly and began to move in circles on it. I was aroused by the feel of it, and of another at my chest, cupping my rounded pec, another slipping to my other side and fastening itself to my nipple. Another hand suddenly there on my calf as I lifted my leg at the shock of the touch. The hand on my belly had moved down now. It pulled at my cock, moved to cup my balls and squeezed them gently. Firmly. I gasped and rolled my hips.

The hand on my calf was now working its way to my inner thigh and I widened my legs for it. My nipple burned from the twisting it had received, and I opened my mouth wide to gulp air in as I arched my back, sending my chest out to meet the cupping, twisting hands. I widened my thighs and bent my legs as another hand slid under my thigh and ran up to my cheek. I lifted my cheek for it and it ran under me.

Large strong fingers slid into my crease, and I landed on them as the hand that had cupped my pec began to pinch that nipple, making me lift myself to that side now. My other nipple was freed, burning and throbbing in sharp little tingles. That hand ran down my body, circling and stroking till it reached my cock and wrapped itself about my hard, throbbing shaft. A finger teased my pisshole, and I moaned. My body was on fire, but I had a touch of fear still.

"Who's there?" I gasped. "Who are you? Stephen? Ohhh," I moaned, as the hand began to stroke my cock and my hips moved. The hand under my cheek kneaded the solid muscle there. I moaned again, hearing myself above the music and the soft rapid breathing of my unknown invisible ravishers. The hand left my cock while another left my balls.

"No," I moaned, "No, don't stop."

Then a hand was sliding under my ass again and pushing me gently up, and rolling me over. I ended on my stomach and was attacked again by hands at my shoulders, fingers tracing the line of my spine. Hands cupping my butt, kneading my cheeks before firm fingers separated them, exposing my asshole to a soft breath of air. I gasped as a wet tongue touched me there, circling my rim.

"Yes," I gasped. "Yes," burying my face in the sheet, rubbing my trapped cock and balls against the sheet.

A hand was at my right thigh. It stroked up my leg to my ass, stroked the line of my butt, the crease between my butt and my thigh. I arched back as the tongue tasted me and another hand ran down my back

"Oh yes," I sighed, "Oh yes."

The tongue left my rim, and I felt a hand, large and strong, there between my cheeks. I pushed back slowly as a thick finger entered me, wanting it now. It sank in and I felt myself let go. Then the finger left briefly, and I gasped and moaned as more filled me, two fingers I knew, two thick fingers.

"Oh, yes, fuck me," I moaned. "Fuck me."

Hands caressed and teased my body for a few more moments, and then I was empty.

"No. No," I cried quietly. "Don't stop." I heard a faint rumble as if someone had wanted to laugh at my begging. "Who's there?" I asked again, demandingly.

I breathed deeply as my body was momentarily untouched. Then the hands were at my hips, lifting me. I rested my head on my arms and lifted my ass. I was spread wide and slick lube was stroked over my entrance and fingered inside me. Then the head of a thick cock was there, and I wanted it inside me. I pushed my ass back to it, but it had to be worked slowly into me.

I hadn't expected a monster, crying out as the thick head worked through my entrance and made its way up. A hand was in my hair, stroking it as I cried out again, turning my head. I felt the heel of a thumb press into my mouth. The huge cock moved in the last inches fast and I gasped and cried out again in pain, my cry cut off by the flesh pressed into my open mouth and I bit down hard on the pad at the base of the thumb. Taking out the pain of being split apart on my hidden unknown fondler.

I released the flesh from my mouth and moaned and tossed my head as the huge cock began to fuck me. It pulled out, then fucked me in short strokes and I spread myself wider. The strokes lengthened, and I cried out raggedly, then whimpered and moaned as the fucking became deep and thrusting. A hand was on my cock, stroking it; another was on my balls, squeezing them lightly. I cried out and arched back, falling forward as my arms reached the limit of their movement. I shot off into the hand enclosing me, then again, and shook from the final deep-driving thrusts of the huge cock that was reaming my gut. I felt my ravisher come deep inside me. Felt him empty me slowly as his long thick weapon slid out.

I slumped forward as I was emptied. Nothing touched me now. Whoever the hands had belonged to, I knew they were gone. All but one pair. I felt the soft material binding my wrists being removed. I lay there on my side and curled my legs to me. A hand came and pushed my bent leg up, and I rolled on to my back, my legs wide apart as I brought my hands to my face and removed the blindfold. I blinked at the bright light as I looked down between my bent spread legs, to see my lover smiling down at me. I wrapped my thighs about his hips and pulled him into me.

He leaned over and I wrapped my arms about him.

"Happy Birthday," he said, before his lips took mine and drew me into a bottomless kiss.

VIEW FROM THE BARN

"You and Clancy can go fishing tomorrow," my father said.

The five of us, Uncle Ted, Aunt Bessie, Clancy, Dad, and I were finishing our afternoon tea in the farmhouse kitchen after unloading the fourth load of hay for the day. It was the last day of the haymaking season, and we'd be bringing in the last load that afternoon. The new corrugated iron shed was now half full of hay bales, and that was all there was room for there, as the rest of it was taken up with the farm machinery. The few horses dad still kept were in the old split log barn, which had seen better days. Dad said that horses would soon be a thing of the past, and the rafters of the old barn were too low for the machinery he had on order, but it took the rest of the hay.

"Sure," I replied, looking across the checked tablecloth at Clancy. "Thanks, Dad," I added sourly.

James Benning and his sister Mary had come by the previous morning to ask me to a tennis party on Sunday. Mary had smiled down at me from her seat up on the buggy, and I would have gone and leaned against the side next to her and looked up into her pretty face and become tongue-tied, if Dad hadn't had his hand resting possessively on my shoulder, holding me next to him.

Dad had told James "no" before I'd had a chance to say anything myself. "Sorry James. But Richard is only here for the few weeks of the holidays, and I need him for the hay cutting and other work."

It wasn't true. I knew that. James and his sister knew that. Once the hay was in there was little extra work to do on the farm. I knew the real reason I was being kept away from the Benning's house was Mary. And it rankled that he didn't trust me. After all, I was nineteen now and living and going to university, in Sydney. I felt I was an adult. But I didn't think to cross him. My brother, Rob, and I had been brought up strictly, and I knew what Rob's death had meant to Dad.

"Do you want to go to Chittaway Bay or the mouth of the creek?" I asked Clancy politely.

'The creek," Clancy replied, smiling across at me with his short, dark-blond hair, wide-open face, and big, white teeth. He was no taller than me and lean and wiry, with strong hands. Not big hands, just good, versatile, working hands. I'd been home over a week, and we'd been working together all that time, but I'd still hardly spoken to Dad's new help.

"What's running?" I asked him, still being polite.

"Reckon something will be," he replied, with a shrug and a smile.

Uncle Ted shouted, "I reckon the prawns might be coming down about now. Take the net with you."

Aunt Bessie's husband, Ted, had gone to the Great War and come home hard of hearing and prone to nightmares and always shouted.

At dawn the next morning, Clancy and I rode off toward the creek, me on my father's good horse and Clancy on Uncle Ted's. But when we left the track to the farm, I almost didn't go off onto the narrower one that led to the

175

creek. I looked up the main track that ran onto the road that eventually passed by the Benning's farm, a mile away. I would much rather have been going there to sit out under the big almond trees with Mary and James. Playing tennis, and talking the way we used to when I was still at school and we were all on holidays. But in the last year things had changed. And I could understand what my father felt, but I could still want things to be different and wish he would start treating me like an adult.

Clancy led the way to a familiar shady patch of grass on the bank of the creek. "I used to come here with my father and Rob, my brother—in the old days," I told him as he dismounted.

"Hmm, with your dad?" Clancy responded, looking up at me, "It was your dad showed it to me, not long ago," he replied, smiling. I vaguely wondered what had made my father's last farmhand, Pete, leave. The young men who came to work for him all seemed to get on with Dad and were treated like part of the family.

After my mother died, trying to give Dad another son, Bessie had arrived to keep house, along with Ted to help around the farm. A few years after, Dad had got himself his first paid help, and since then there had been a series of fit, young men who'd come and gone. Some staying a few months, some a couple of years. Ours was one of the bigger farming properties in the Gosford area.

When we'd unpacked the fishing gear, Clancy waded into the muddy brown water of the wide creek, with the throw net, and cast it out into deeper water. Standing still and watching as it settled to the muddy bottom, before he pulled it in, rapidly and smoothly. When it came out of the water, I could see the handful of golden prawns, trapped and struggling inside the mesh.

"Hey, Ted was right," Clancy yelled, laughing as he brought the net ashore. We picked out the spiky, kicking catch and transferred them to the billy can, which I had filled with water as soon as I knew the prawns were coming in.

We filled the billy to the top with prawns, to take back home, then set out our fishing lines and lay back to wait for whatever happened.

"Mind my line," I said to Clancy not long after we'd settled down, "I need to go."

I wandered along to a nearby tree and unbuttoned my fly. When I was finished and shaking out the last drops, I nearly jumped out of my skin. Until he spoke I hadn't realized Clancy was standing beside me, looking down. "Can I feel you?" Clancy asked in such a quiet, polite way that I was too amazed to stop him, and he reached out and wrapped his fingers around my dick and rubbed the pad of his thumb over my knob.

"Yeuhhh," I hissed at the feel of what his fingers were doing on me, my young body responding instantly to his experienced touch.

Then I wasn't facing the tree anymore, and Clancy had knelt down in front of me. I was even more overwhelmed as he wrapped his lips around my dick head, moving it into his mouth sucking on me, and doing some tongue work. Moving his mouth down my fast stiffening shaft and back up again.

If I hadn't been in total shock at what was happening, I would have pushed him away, buttoned myself up, and told him I was going home. Probably saying that if he ever tried anything like that again, I'd tell my father, and he'd be out of a job.

But I didn't do any of that. I just stood there, gaping and looking down at Clancy's dark, blond head bobbing up and down, as my cock filled out and throbbed under his attentions. Then I heard a groan, my groan. I was gripping his hair and jerking his head back and forth, faster and faster. Moaning, faster and faster. Until I came. Stunned to be filling his mouth with my cum.

It was 1938. I had never even seen a woman naked, much less played around with one. I had heard whispered stories about what men sometimes did with each other, but that was in another world. Not my world. Until that afternoon—when I came inside another person for the first time, and it was Clancy's throat I filled with my seed. But as my cock had throbbed and spouted, in my head an image of Mary had swum around. Mary, the shapely form of her body, in her best dress at the Armistice Day picnic the year before, smiling up at me. Lying back on the rug the three of us, James, Mary, and I, had spread under a tree a short distance from the adults.

I looked down, and it was Clancy looking up at me, smiling. "You have a beautiful dick," he said, still holding it. I was embarrassed. And I wondered if I had made some sign that I had wanted what Clancy had given me. If I was sick.

"Hu, uh" I mumbled, stepping back and turning away and pushing myself back into my pants. Buttoning them up as my head swam. I was panting still and feeling . . . well . . . it was infinitely better than when I stroked myself off. I still worried that was a bad thing to do. But I'd never been able to stop myself from doing it.

My head was still spinning a while later as we packed up. I occasionally glanced over at Clancy, wondering that he seemed so normal still. That night in my bed I took my erect dick in my hand and thought of girls, of Mary, but I couldn't help remembering how good Clancy's mouth had felt on me. And I was sure that what had happened was wrong, but I knew I wanted to feel it again. And in my mind, it was Clancy's mouth I was filling when I came.

A couple of days later we were finished with tidying the fields, cutting the last small straggling patch of hay that Dad had considered leaving there for the cows. And while Dad and Uncle Ted stayed with the machinery, Clancy and I took the half-wagon load of hay back to the farm alone.

When the two of us had got it stacked in the old split log barn, we washed up in the horse trough and sat down on a feed sack spread on the hay bales to rest, and wait for Aunt Bessie to call us in for lunch.

"Hey," Clancy said, moving closer to me. "Can I feel your dick again?"

His hands were unbuttoning my fly before I could make myself say anything in reply. I just lay my head back against the hay and looked up at the barn roof, as he freed my already-growing cock and wrapped his lips around it. I moved my hips instinctively. God, he had good lips. Firm, and soft, and full. I moaned as I felt them slide down my stiffening shaft, and I grunted as he teased my knob with his tongue. "Oh, God," I gasped as he took me right in, and I moved my legs apart, and raised and lowered my hips, without even thinking of what I was doing.

When he had me throbbing and moaning he lifted his head and whispered it. "Would you like to put it inside me? Like with a girl?" he asked, in his calm, quiet voice.

I would have put it anywhere just then. I wanted it in him, and pulled his head down till he had me encased again. Giving a few pumps of my hips, I drove myself in and out of that soft sucking mouth, quickly giving him another load of my semen.

But I wondered later, as I lay on my bed with my hand encasing my throbbing cock, how good it must be to put my dick inside a girl.

I thought, "If his mouth is so good, then how much better it must be to have it in the right hole. The one God had meant for it. Or—or in another hole." And I had a thought that maybe if Clancy offered again, I'd ask him what he meant.

When Friday night came round, we all sat in the parlor as usual and listened to Aunt Bessie play the piano. Dad sang a couple of old Scottish songs, and Clancy sang the latest version of "Waltzing Matilda" before Bessie started playing her favorites—Mr. Strauss's waltzes.

Dad was soon snoring, and Ted was doing his best to finish another bottle of beer, so I wandered out onto the veranda for some fresh air, and in a few moments Clancy joined me. We stood in silence for a while, but with me heating up just having him standing there, and with that question on my mind.

"What you were saying . . ." I began hesitantly, but my dick wasn't hesitating,; it was already starting to move and get uncomfortable. "What you were saying about . . . um, girls," I mumbled.

"Come over to the new barn," he said and wandered off in that direction.

I followed him. Already keyed up. Wanting to know what it was like to bury my manhood in someone else's body. Not just a mouth, the real thing. And my hand went to my growing erection and eased it into a more comfortable position in my pants.

Inside the barn Clancy lit a hurricane lamp and hung it by the stack of hay where some bales had been pulled down and set up like a bench and covered with feed bags. He sat down and smiled at me and opened his arms to welcome me to him, in a gesture that became familiar to me. And I stepped into his willing embrace, where I was helping him to unbutton my pants, pulling my cock free, and pressing it to his lips.

I still thought of Mary, and I am sure I was aroused by her, but I was also hungry for the reality of Clancy. Clancy with his soft obliging mouth. Convenient and experienced.

When I was throbbing and not all that far from shooting another load of my semen into his throat, Clancy pushed me gently back.

"You wanna do this like I was a girl?" he asked, smiling up at me dreamily. And I saw that his hand was

180

stroking at his pants and that he had an erection of his own down there.

I had seen his long penis with its loose foreskin a couple of days before, and he had asked me if I wanted to touch it. I had been shocked at the idea and only touched it gingerly. Then he had put it away without seeming upset that I hadn't done for him what he had done for me. And I had been relieved. It was something I was afraid of, of doing to him what he was doing to me. Selfish of me, maybe. But natural.

Now I realized that he really liked what he was doing. And I felt maybe as if I didn't have to feel so guilty, taking what he gave without giving back. As he was also giving himself a good time.

He unbuttoned his fly and slipped off his suspenders, and his pants and underwear dropped to the dirt floor and he stepped out of them. His dick was now standing up, long and thin, with a red bulb on it that seemed to be waving at me, fascinating me. His body was covered in curly dark gold hair, and the skin hidden under his clothes was as white as milk, compared to his deeply tanned arms, face, and neck.

"You can do me in the ass," he said, turning around and leaning over the hay and resting his chest down on it. "Just put some spit on," he added, reaching around his own spit-covered fingers and pressing them in and around his hole, wetting it down and opening it some. He fingers seemed to enter it easily, and I added some of my own spit, which he helped me rub in, and then I was pressing the head of my cock into him as he pulled his cheeks apart.

His entrance was tighter than I had expected. I had imagined I'd just slide on in with no effort, but for a moment it was not so easy, and I wondered if I was doing it right. Then I got in a small way and just sort of glided in the rest. I moaned at the feel of his passage encasing and stroking my moving rod, as it went to its full depth inside him, and my black pubic hair mingled with the dark-gold hair around his entrance.

"Oh gee, Oh," I moaned and sighed, as I plowed him. First slowly, getting my balance, then faster and faster, and harder. I got heated up fast. Ready to burst and pounding my hips against his milky white bum, gripping his hips and jerking as I shot my semen into him.

"Ouff," I grunted. And, "Ouff," and, "Ouff," again, as I let loose of my load in three shots.

Then I collapsed, panting, over his back. I could feel him moving rhythmically under me and realized he was stroking himself off, and I lay there against his body till I heard the sigh and felt him jerk as he came across the hay. I lay there a bit longer, with my hands kneading his shoulders and running over his back and through his hair.

"Thanks," I mumbled, as I stood up and slipped the last way out of him.

Some juice oozed out of his gaping hole, and I was fascinated by it and touched it before he stood up, smiled at me, and came in and hugged me and whispered "That was terrific" in my ear, squeezing me tight.

I went back to the house and into the lounge room, while Clancy went around the back to the kitchen. Inside I found that my father had already gone to bed and Bessie was playing some sad, slow romantic piece, while Ted was lying back on the sofa and singing along unintelligibly. I said good night and made my way unsteadily up to my room, where I fell into bed and was asleep in moments.

That was only the first time I fucked Clancy, and after the second time, I started to reach under him and help him stroke off his long, thin cock in time with my fucking.

For the next few weeks Clancy sucked me off or I fucked him, regularly. Then it was the end of January and the church picnic to celebrate the last weekend before the local schools went back. We piled into my father's car— Bessie, Ted, Clancy my father, and me—and drove to

Gosford to the park on the water. And I saw Mary. It was the first time I had seen her since she and James had come by our place in that first week I was home. With Bessie hovering beside me, I was able to go up and talk to her, and I saw quickly that there was something different about her. James was reserved, but Mary was gushing and laughing as if she had been missing me badly, and if I had seen her like that a few weeks earlier, I might have been spellbound by her, as my father had feared. But I had changed too. My first nine months studying in Sydney, and the time since I had come home for summer, had changed me forever.

On that day I found Mary not as appealing as I always had. There was something rough about her that I hadn't ever seen before. Something in the way she giggled and rolled her eyes, and leaned over so I could get a glimpse of her breasts down the front of her dress, that was alien to the young women my great aunt had been introducing me to in Sydney. And Mary talked of nothing but tennis parties and who had been at picnics I'd missed.

When Rob was alive, there had been no plans for me, and no one minded that I was taken with Mary. Her family had a good-sized property, and if I chose to marry her and stay on the farm, that was fine. It was hoped that either Rob or I would go to Sydney and join my great uncle in the legal profession. He had his own practice. But it didn't matter to my father which one of us did. Then I had been standing on the frame of the new tractor beside Rob, as he sat in the seat and drove it, when he had run it too fast up a small rise, and it had flipped over. Now he was gone, and I had a damaged leg. And my father had decided that my future was in the law, not in the physically demanding work of the farm.

I could see now that Mary could never be the wife for me in my Sydney future, and not just because of what it was rumored might have happened while I had been away. I was polite and said I'd missed her, but as we talked, I could see by the look in her eyes that she realized I was lying. Her mouth became a trembling line, her eyes frightened and teary. James stepped in then, and pushing me aside, he led her away.

I rejoined the adults and found the talk was all of the threat of Hitler and another war in Europe. And when we got home that night, Ted was more than half drunk and alternated shouting, "There is going to be another bloody war. Damn them to hell. All of them," with sobbing loudly.

My father looked grim for some reason and disappeared up to his room early, while Clancy read the newspaper on the kitchen table. I wandered out to the new barn and lit the lamp; half hoping Clancy would follow me. I wandered around the machinery for a few minutes, then climbed the ladder up into the loft and lay down on the hay, looking out of the tall, narrow window in the end wall. Looking up at the clear night sky and considering how much I had moved away from the life and people of the place I had grown up in. And of what another war would mean to my world.

Lights were on in the house. We had the electricity connected—but no close neighbors, so on hot nights the windows would be wide open, with no curtains drawn across them to interrupt the breeze. There was a good distance between me and the house, but some movement in my father's room drew my attention to it, and I focused on it, brooding still on other things, before I realized that there were two white figures in there. With shock I recognized who they were, both pale bodied and naked. Focusing on them properly, I saw one reach out his arms in a familiar welcoming gesture and go down on his knees before the other and move his face into his dark haired groin.

I was both mesmerized and horrified. I realized I was watching Clancy go down and suck on my father's penis as he had sucked on mine. I remembered the feel of Clancy's soft mouth on my dick, and I couldn't stop myself

184

releasing my own cock from my pants and stroking it. And while watching Clancy mount my father on his bed and slide that long thin cock of his up my father's ass I stroked myself to my ejaculation. I confess I stayed there in the barn window and watched all they did with each other, until they were done, and the light went out.

Fortunately, I was going back to Sydney in a couple of days, and I managed to avoid being alone with Clancy again. But I was embarrassed whenever I was with my father, and more so when I saw the two of them go off together to the new barn and not return till Bessie called them in for lunch.

I returned to Sydney with a hundred thoughts in my head. Why my father had never remarried. Why Clancy had given himself to me so readily. Home was suddenly a mass of confusion, but within months the war had started, and I was conveniently kept too busy in Sydney to make it back to the farm again for a couple of years.

When I did return, it was to find little changed. Clancy had not been accepted into the army and had stayed on the farm. My father seemed content, and there was a new tractor in the corrugated iron barn. I was determined not to accept any overtures that Clancy might make but was disappointed not to have my resolve tested when he made none. He did nothing to suggest anything had ever happened between us, or happened between him and my father. And sitting there at the dinner table with Bessie, Ted, Clancy, and my father, I found it hard to believe that anything ever had.

Clancy never left the farm, and when my father died, he left him a life tenancy of it.

VISITING A NEIGHBOR

It was the deep darkness of a moonless night as I crept through the open glass doors from the rooftop patio into the open bedroom. I was barely able to see the bed and slid my feet carefully across the unfamiliar floor as I made my way toward it. Then I froze as I heard the sound of movement and observed a bunching in the dark shadow of the bed. I hesitated about continuing, not wanting to be discovered,

It had been three months since I had first seen him climbing the staircase at the corner of his house. I had been glancing out of my window on a hot evening and had noticed the unfamiliar flickering image of a man walking upstairs behind the glass brick stairwell wall. I would not have seen him if it had not been dark and his house and the stairwell had not been so well lit, but I was immediately captivated by the shimmering broken image of a gracefully moving body. He moved smoothly and easily as he climbed and he was obviously straight and lean and tanned. He was a golden shimmer going—to where—I wondered, to his bedroom?

I observed him often after that and noted, with some difficulty without the benefit of the internal lights, that in the mornings he made the same naked trip down the stairs. I had become fascinated by my new neighbor. I took to walking along the street in the mornings and again in the evenings and once saw a man emerge from his house who I thought must be him. Another time I saw another man enter it, but he was not my neighbor I knew. He was wiry and blond, and though good looking, did not move anything like my neighbor did. But I hesitated there deep in thought, and it was then I saw through the frosted glass door that inside he embraced another man and they were locked together for some time before moving from my sight.

After that vision I became even more obsessed, and I had time on my hands. In that hot Mediterranean city, the flat roof of my house connected to another, which connected to another. Eventually—if I jumped a narrow alleyway, the roofs led to my stair-climbing neighbor's rooftop patio. My first trip there gave me a lot to think about, but I returned home after doing no more than proving I could get there when I wanted.

Now here I was, standing in his bedroom in the dark, afraid he'd wake. The shadowy bed was still again and I resumed my careful silent approach to it. My eyes were adjusted to the gloom now, and as I got closer, I began to make out his body lying there. When I stood near enough for my knees to touch his sheet I looked down at him in fascination.

He was long and lean and well defined, the faint shadows showing his muscles as a pattern of ridges and mounds that I followed over his chest and arms and spread thighs as I ran my eyes over his sleeping body. The dark shadow of his pubic hair was visible at his crotch, broken by the pale mass of his soft, but surprisingly long, hairless flesh. I greedily gazed my fill, but in the shadows of the room, he remained more of an impression than a body I could memorize and recognize in daylight. I hoped that I would also be unrecognizable.

Finally, I leaned over, and in a moment had covered his body with mine. He jerked awake under me, and I felt how strong he was as he yelled out, "Hey, get off me. Get out of here. Bastard."

I grabbed for his hands, but he was trying to roll me away, and I had trouble finding them. Then he hit me hard. I now became serious in my efforts to contain and control him. His legs squirmed about between mine, and I clamped my thighs tight about his as he somehow got the leverage to roll over and take me with him. I was fighting for his arms and grunting with the effort I made as he fought and kicked and shouted, "Who are you?" "Get off me." "Get out of here."

His breathing was coming in ever-more-rapid gasps. "Stop it, or you'll get hurt," I said to him. "Stop this."

But we were two men wrestling for control, and our legs were now wrapped about each other's, my thighs rubbing against the outside of his as my chest and stomach slid across his. I grasped one wrist and made a grab for his other one.

I could feel his hard tool now. We were both hard from the fear and the naked wrestling we were doing in the darkness. Suddenly, he had rolled on top of me again and I made a great effort and twisted my legs and flipped him back onto his back, with me momentarily having control of his arms and thighs and feeling his hard cock buried between the muscles of our straining thighs and stomachs. I took the chance to find his open, panting mouth with mine, to force a kiss from him. He was stunned for a moment, before he resumed the struggle, but now it was with his tongue fighting with my tongue inside his warm mouth, with its muscular lips and big teeth.

I could feel his engorged cock pressing against my own, and I strained again to wrap my legs about his thighs and immobilize him.

But he was suddenly more occupied by our kiss than I was, fighting me inside his mouth. I relaxed my thighs and instead reached for his cock in the dark and, finding it, gripped it and worked it briefly. This distracted him more, so that his mouth and hands relaxed and he had suddenly allowed himself to be possessed by me. I moved my legs to free his, and he spread them wide. I felt his hand at my throbbing cock as I reached behind him and slid my fingers between his cheeks and touched his entrance briefly. He quivered and I further relaxed my grip on him. He opened his left leg out and lifted it to wrap around my back, opening himself wide for me. I needed no further invitation and in a moment had buried my finger in his entrance. He moaned "More," as his kissing became more frenzied.

I roughly fed him another finger. "Yes," he gasped, and I fed him another, feeling his rim tighten as he tensed. He cried out, releasing my mouth, and moved his other leg out wider, curling it about my thigh and opening himself further. I twisted what I had inside him, rotating my fingers roughly as far in as I could force them. "Yes," he gasped, arching back. "That's good," he hissed, and then he was kissing me again.

But I pulled his upper leg away and pushed it up to him and found him surprisingly flexible, so that I nestled my hips between his thighs and drilled my fingers deeper into his body while my cock rubbed about against his cock and his belly. He was starting to produce some lubrication and his rim was loosening on my buried fingers. Then he was wriggling under me. "I want your cock," he said, "inside me." I let him lift his legs high and wide, and he stroked himself as I took my engorged rod and forced it inside him.

189

He cried out and moaned repeatedly, stroking himself until he came as I finally bottomed in him. Then he groaned loudly as I started plowing him. I plowed him till he was ready to come again. I felt his body clenching and arching as he came, which sent me over the edge too.

"Stay inside me," he moaned once I'd come in him "Stay there."

I moved him and rolled him over on his side without slipping out, and he lay there with my arms about his chest. Pulling his face back to mine for another slow kiss, he gave me possession of his mouth.

He was an obliging lover, and I took advantage of it, fucking him deeply again when I was ready. He moaned and gave me encouraging little sighs and little repeated whispered encouragements of "Yes," "Fuck me deeper," "Yes, like that."

When he finally dozed off, I eased myself out of him and off the bed, and I slipped back out onto the roof and away. I returned to my house and slept deeply, only waking to watch him descend his staircase in the morning. He was moving differently to the way he'd moved the morning before, and I wondered how he would move the next morning, after another night visit from me.

Later in the day I happened to have to deliver some papers to him in his office, and he looked up as he smiled an acknowledgment, his eyes shadowed with tiredness and not giving any hint of recognition.

WHIFF OF TEMPTATION

I gave up smoking ten years ago, for the second time, after keeping off it for six years from the previous time. And it was worse than hard to do that second time, and I know I couldn't do it again. Even now my brain still starts craving tobacco whenever I smell the sweet aroma of fresh tobacco, fresh cigarettes. Even the fresh smoke exhaled across a table. Ahhhhhhh, yes. I only have to smell really good fresh tobacco smoke for my body to start whatever the smoking equivalent is of salivating. Slobbering in a lustful urge to . . . inhale.

Uhhum. So, I try to avoid places people smoke, and smokers. I am also very sensitive to the smell and taste of stale smoke now, and I can't stick my tongue in the mouth of someone who smokes. And I don't want their stale, tar-coated one in mine either, thank you.

My friends and lovers are now nonsmokers. Which is fine, as it also means that they are healthier, will live and love longer, have more disposable income, and well, lots of other good things that go with being a nonsmoker.

So, it was quite a shock and very worrying when I started to get a whiff of the smell of tobacco smoke when I visited them. All of a sudden the heady aroma of really good tobacco was everywhere, and it all started at a party Morris had one night—not a real party, but maybe ten people, some wine and a BBQ under the new pergola in his recently replanted garden.

I had to be at work at 6:00 AM the next morning, so I left the party early just as the evening started to warm up, saying, "bye" to Neil, Arnold, Morris and Colin, Dave, and the rest of them. Ah well, I've got to make a living. But as I was leaving, a wave of rich tobacco smoke wafted past me, and I was almost knocked over by it. I turned to see who it was, but all I saw was the unfamiliar back of a well-built guy with dark hair and a trail of smoke drifting up from in front of him as he walked out to the garden where the BBQ was. And I was stunned to see Morris, who was also a reformed smoker and was now obsessive about not getting the smell of smoke in his furnishings, rush forward and embrace the new arrival in a gush of half-heard words.

It wasn't the smell of an ordinary cigarette that had come off the stranger I knew, but I didn't give it much thought at the time; I was just very surprised he was there and glad to be escaping the seductive aroma.

The next day was Saturday, and after work I stopped by to pick Neil up and take him to the gym. We always worked out together on Saturdays and Tuesdays, and I was surprised not to find him waiting at the door for me. But then again sometimes he worked on the weekends and sometimes I'd find him asleep on his sofa recovering from Friday night. Since the door was wide open, I wandered in and took a bottle of Staminade from his fridge. But there was a strange smell, and as I stood up and opened the bottle, I sniffed and suddenly I was hit by the smell of that tobacco again. The same one as at Morris's, rich and pungent. In shock, I wondered what it was doing there and where Neil was.

Muffled noises drew me further into the house, and I wandered on, the smell of tobacco growing stronger, leading me to Neil's open bedroom door. On the bed I saw, and heard, the reason Neil had forgotten about getting ready for the gym.

Neil was on his knees, and I could see his smooth thighs sitting wide outside another pair of solid muscular thighs coated in a light coat of dark, curly hair. Yes, behind him and pumping his ass was what I was sure was the body of the dark-haired, well-built guy I'd last seen at Morris's, whose hairless muscular butt cheeks were now clenching and releasing as he pumped my moaning gym buddy's ass.

The aroma of his cigar circled around me. Because I now knew that was what the smell was—a cigar. Yes, the stranger's thick cigar butt sat on a plate on the bedside chest as its owner fucked my reformed smoker, gym buddy, Neil.

Their moans and grunts had led me there, and Neil was moaning more loudly now and writhing under his attacker, as the guy did some gyrating and shallow stroking inside my mate's channel that had me wishing it was me he had there on the bed. I love a guy who can really work his cock around in my ass and reach every part of it, but that thinking was doing me no good. Because the aroma of the tobacco had me starting to salivate. I had to get out of there fast.

So, I escaped, half hard and filled with the desire for a good fuck. But also afraid—because even in the brief time I had been in Neil's house, I had been starting to yearn for the rich tobacco aroma and had been taking deep breaths to suck it into my lungs, ahhh, and slowly exhaling. I'd had to get out of there. Whatever the hunky dark-haired guy was smoking was like a drug to me.

Outside I took big gulps of fresh air and told myself it was much better, cleaner, sweeter, all that, so much more enjoyable than the smell of tobacco. And I also tried to convince myself that the cigar smoker's butt, thighs, back, and other body parts were not doing anything for me. I could not get myself hooked on a smoker.

"And he's Neil's," I told myself firmly.

At the gym I worked out hard, breathed deeply, and complained to Garth how hard it could be to stay off them, even ten years after I had given up cigarettes. He agreed. He'd been there too. So by the time I headed home, I had got my lust for the cigar-smoking stranger and his aromatic cigars out of my system.

"So did you . . . um, come by yesterday? On your way to the gym?" Neil asked hesitatingly that evening when he called me.

"Yep," I said, "And, yep, I smelt it. The smoke. And I saw what was keeping you too busy to notice the time," I said bluntly. "He's a smoker. Geez, Neil."

"Yeah," he laughed, "Well. Don't sound so stuffy. Sorry, but you know it's been a while and I couldn't turn down a hunky guy who wants to fuck, and man, that was a great one."

"The guy smokes," I said, "All the time."

"Yeah, well, I can handle it."

"But, Neil," I said in exasperation, "I spent six months listening to you moaning how you were dying for a smoke while you wore patches and had injections and hypnosis."

I had been through more hell than Neil, I was sure. Being a successful "giver upper," I had babied several friends though the drama of giving up smoking.

"He imports them. Luca, the Latin hunk. Genuine, hand-rolled Cuban cigars made on the sweaty thighs of testosterone-loaded young Cuban men. And . . . and," he stopped and giggled, then whispered, "And you have no idea, Steve, how many things he can do with a cigar."

Geezus, dream on, Neil, I thought, but he was saying it all with real lust in his voice, whether for the guy or his cigars I had no idea.

"And you know cigars are not as bad for you as cigarettes. Cigars have less nicotine and are organic," Neil added.

"Neil," I shouted down the phone, "Don't you dare."

On Sunday I was having lunch with Arnold and his sister at the Aqua Café on the waterfront. Lots of fresh air and great views of the lake. I walked down there sucking in the sweet warm air of summer and thinking about sex. Particularly about solid, muscular thighs with a fine coat of black, curly hair, topped by a hair-free pumping butt and imagining a nice seven incher nearby. Sigh. I tried to change the image. This was bad.

Arnold and Lydia were late, and I got a nasty shock when we finished our Thai beef salads. I hadn't smelt it on him as we were outdoors, but suddenly Arnold had to get up and cross the pavement, and I watched in shock as he pulled out a pack of cigarettes and lit one and dragged hard on it. I was stunned.

"But . . . he gave up, years ago," I said, gaping at him.

"Don't talk about it," his sister, Lydia, snapped. "I have already yelled at him, but he's hooked already. It's that bloody Luca he's been dating. God, he's a hunk, but he's got a cigar in his hand the whole time and leaves one behind every time he visits," She said angrily. "But of course one cigar isn't enough, he was a two-pack-a-day man when he gave up, and he's already back on to a pack a day"

"Luca?" I asked. "But, um . . ." I wasn't quite sure how to tell Lydia that the dark hunk was also fucking Neil. "The guy seems to be a one-man conversion to smoking campaign," I said, frowning.

Arnold had had a lump removed from a lung and given up in a panic. Gone cold-turkey. I had never expected him to take up smoking again. He came back to the table looking sheepish, and lunch was spoiled. Lydia and I both glared at him, and he reacted by telling us how good a fucker his new boyfriend was.

There wasn't much I could say to that. I knew he was good. I'd seen him in action. I just shook my head at the end of lunch and said; "If you want to die for a good fuck, Arnold, well, don't expect us to come running with the fruit and sympathy when you are in hospital with lung cancer." I was brutal, I know, but we all knew what his family history was—his father and two uncles dead of lung cancer, and what his specialist had said.

On Tuesday I went to pick up Neil, and I could smell it—smoke—but it wasn't the rich aroma that came from a hand-rolled Cuban cigar, spun off some nubile youths' sweaty thigh. More like the stale smell of Alpine menthol.

"What? No way. I haven't had a smoke, promise," he said when I confronted him on it, but he didn't look me in the eye.

I dropped him off after the gym, and he didn't ask me in for a drink like usual. I knew why. He couldn't have a nicotine fix if I was there. I sighed and drove off. Damn Luca, I thought. What was he, some one-man devil's helper? Or perhaps he had been let loose on the gay community by Phillip Morris now that AIDS was waning.

That night I dreamed of those bare butt-cheeks and imagined the cigar man pumping my ass amid a haze of smoke. I woke up sweating. The guy, Luca, was spoiling my sex life.

Ok. I lusted for him, but the cigars—well, they terrified me, and I had no idea if I could resist him, and them. I certainly couldn't have him without succumbing to the other. Fortunately, he was Arnold's date. Well, supposedly.

On Friday night I went to meet Morris; his other half, Colin; and Neil for dinner in town at Goldbergs'. It was busy as usual, and I was heading to their table when I

196

realized that "he" was the guy with his back to me sitting on the other side of Neil. And the faint smell of fine aromatic tobacco was in the air.

"Shit," I said out loud and moved around the table so that I was opposite him and took the empty chair next to Morris. But as I sat down, I could smell smoke again, stale, ordinary cigarette smoke, and it was coming from Morris. I leaned closer and sniffed. Yes, it was Morris. I felt the blood drain from my body. God, Morris, and Neil and Arnold. Who was next? Me?

No, not me too, I thought. At last I got to see Luca's face, and that was no help at all. What his rear view had promised, his front view delivered. Dark, smoldering eyes, masculine Latin features and good looks. He flashed a smile at me—all white teeth and big mouth. I hated him.

Shit, I thought silently. Shit.

"How's Arnold?" I demanded, suddenly seeing red and looking directly at Luca.

"Arnold? He is well, last time I saw him."

"He's smoking again," I shouted. I wanted my anger to overcome my desire. "He's had a lump removed from a lung. He has a family history of lung cancer, and he should never smoke again." I fixed the hunky Luca with a steely gaze, sending waves of hate at him. Well, attempting too.

"Oh," he said, suddenly looking sad. "No, I didn't know that. But he is an adult; he should know what he can do."

I laughed at that idea. "Ha. I laugh at that idea. What, some hunky Latin with a big cock fucks him to paradise and he's going to act like an adult?" I asked. "And you leave him cigars?"

"You and Arnold?" Neil said, looking at Luca, "You are dating Arnold too?"

"Yes, and why not? I am not monogamous, I am not married to anyone," Luca said, waving a hand nonchalantly about.

"That pudgy, pale guy?" Neil demanded more loudly, "You are dating him?" Neil looked stunned, and I could understand why. Neil was the product of good genes and ten years of hard training. He was a superb specimen, and he was fussy about the quality of who got to play with the goods. I'd never quite made the grade, though I had lusted after him badly to begin with.

But I wasn't going to let Neil distract me from venting my anger at Luca. "And how about you behave like an adult. Be an adult and stop encouraging everyone you fuck to smoke," I added, knowing I was ruining the party and feeling like some religious maniac on a soapbox, but also feeling I had a right to be angry.

People in the café were looking our way now.

"Fucking and smoking are the great pleasures in my life," Luca replied, his eyes hooded and flashing at me. "I fuck many; young, old, handsome, strong, rich men. Many things about a man attract me. But what I like best is a man who has real passion. True passion is rare," he added seeming to stare at me.

"You fuck many? Old? Rich? Well, fuck you," shouted Neil angrily, standing up so his chair fell back with a loud crash. "Fuck you," he spat at Luca. "Are you coming?" he threw at me, and I knew I should leave. A good-looking guy with a cigar looked at me and I was a wreck, in lust and heat. But at least I wasn't smoking again, and I left with Neil.

When we arrived at his place, Neil dragged me inside. "Here. Here," he said, rushing through the house and throwing an opened packet of cigarettes at me, then an unopened pack and matches and a lighter and a bag of butts and ash. "Get rid of them for me. Please."

I threw them in the rubbish bin in the park over the road and came back to find Neil was waiting for me, panting, with his eyes flashing. "No one has ever done anything for me like you have, Steve," he said. "I mean that.

198

No one. And there is one thing that stops me wanting a cigarette, and I know you wanted it once. So I'm hoping you'll help me give it up again. Will you, Steve? Do you still want it? Say, yes," he begged, holding my hand and looking into my eyes.

I was a bit lost, actually. "Um, of course," I said, though I wasn't sure what he expected me to do.

But then he grabbed my arm and dragged me to his bedroom, and my heart skipped a dozen regular beats to jump about like a hooked fish as I realized he was going to give himself to me. My cock lurched and I was ripping his T off him before he had even unzipped his jeans. I was rock hard by the time my pants got kicked off and we fell onto the bed together.

"Oh god, you don't know. . . ," I babbled, grabbing his face and slapping my lips to his. His arms were running over me like hot liquid as our tongues fought for dominance, and our bodies rubbed against each other in a frenzy of heat trying to merge. Hands reaching for cocks, mouths straining to reach chests and necks.

Somehow his mouth ended up wrapped around my rod, and I was spreading his cheeks and fingering his butt and sucking his balls.

He rubbed his dick between his belly and my chest in a slow, small fucking motion as I opened his ass with my fingers. Then I gave up his nuts and my tongue reached in to him. Wetting and digging into that tight, puckered opening I was going to plow soon, if he didn't make me come first.

In one natural smooth motion, he gave up my rod and rolled over, and I rolled between his spread thighs and was kneeling back with his butt on my thighs and holding the head of my cock to his hole. I played my cock head around his rim, stroking over it and back, watching it twitch; then I had a finger inside making him gape and pressed my rod in.

"Oh baby," I moaned, as he enclosed my dick inside him. "Oh yes."

The finger came out, and my hand went to stroking his tool as I worked into his ass between his moans and whimpers. I wasn't that long, but I was thick. And I let loose years of pent-up lust and desire in fucking him deep and hard as he begged and encouraged me. He had somehow managed to roll a rubber on me in our frenzy, and my only regret in that first wild joining was that I filled the rubber instead of sending my seed shooting into every part of his being, taking possession of every cell of his body. I milked him as I pumped the last of my cum inside him, joining and merging me to him, watching his cream spout and fall on his chest and face and up the bed.

Then I collapsed over him, totally spent, and we rolled into each other and I cradled his butt in my lap and his back to my chest. I sighed in satisfaction, and realized I wouldn't have minded a cigarette, and shuddered. There must have been some faint smell in the air of his bedroom still that was activating my salivary glands. But the urge died fast as I started to engorge again and played with his filling cock. Yes, fucking was definitely a good distraction.

"So, how long do you think we need to do this to cure you?" I asked him, nuzzling his ear and reaching the point of my tongue inside it.

"Oh years and years, I reckon," He replied.

At work a week later I got a phone call. I picked the phone up, smiling, thinking it would be Neil, for the third time that day, but it wasn't.

"Hi Steve, it's Luca," an incredibly sexy deep voice was saying, "I would really like to met up with you. To get to know you better, to become friends."

"What? Luca, you smoke," I replied, "And I have a guy in my life," I added, feeling warm at the thought of Neil waiting for me when I got home that night.

"I have given up the cigars. Just for you, Steve. There are so few men of passion and you have passion, Steve. I want to fuck you. Since the day at the café, I have thought of nothing else. That evening I gave them up. No cigars for a week. For you I have even done that. That is why I have called only now. So you would know that I am serious in my feelings."

"You have given up smoking?" I said, suddenly flushed with surprise that I had had that affect on a hunk like him. And the voice brought back memories of his face and body and those glutes flexing and relaxing and . . .

It wouldn't have taken Neil six months to give up smoking if he wasn't a man of fixed habits, and he was now including my favorite ice cream on his shopping list and I was happy.

But Luca? I mean no one gives up smoking in a couple of hours because he fancies a man. Or does he? "For me?" I asked, "You have really given up because of me?"

"Yes, for you, Steve. So tonight we meet. Yes? I want your butt in my hands, to spread your cheeks, see your hole twitch for me, your cock grow and throb . . ."

It was tempting. Listening to Luca, I was very tempted.

"Sorry," I said, "But I'm taken." And the truth was that once I had fucked Neil, I was hooked on him. I also have an addictive personality.

But I'll confess that I didn't hang up the phone on Luca. Because I knew that if he tried a bit harder—well, I might just manage to find a good excuse to get home late one evening.

~

ABOUT THE AUTHOR

Sabb lives in Australia by a lake. Once he was an accountant and occasionally a property developer, now he is relaxing, but he has always been a wild barbarian at heart. He has too many dogs and works out at the gym as much as he can.

And he knows that love is out there, somewhere, you just have to be lucky enough to find it. He is very grateful he has found it.

Not all books listed below may currently be on release.
* indicates the book is available in paperback and e-book.
BOOKS BY CHRIS CROSS
Multisexual Adult Romance
Pulaski Square
BOOKS BY ALEX LOCKHEED
Transgender Romance

Meeting Jenna
Transgender Other
Being Sarah
BOOKS BY DIRK HESSIAN
Xtreme Historical Erotica
The King's Men
Shores of Tripoli
Prophecy of Noto
Pretender's Fate
General Historical Erotic Romance
To the Hessian Hills
Fire Down the Valley*
Constantinople*
The Beautiful Way*
Blue and Gray
Colonel's Treasure
Beginning of Time
Labyrinth
BOOKS BY HABU
Gay Erotica
Memoir Faction
Flying High, Diving Deep*
Xtreme Erotica
Tramp Steaming*
Escape to Girne
Silas' Choice*
Last Call
Choke Hold
Apyko: The Greek Pimp
Visits of the Schlange
Second Coming: Emile La Cour Unleashed
Vortex: Sacrificed by Curiosity*
Dark Angel Sounding *(in e-book & included in
Sounding:Ultimate Control Paperback)*
Sounding: Ultimate Control (*Print Only*)*
Sounding Five *(in e-book & included in
Sounding:Ultimate Control paperback)*
Romance

Turn to Love
Rain Check
Built for Pleasure (Sci Fi)
Danny's Choice*
Pull of the Groove
Sugar n Spice Christmas
Friday Nights with Lenny (Christmas Romance)
Snowy, Snowy Nights (Christmas Romance)
Tank n Bull
Sail to the Sun
War Letters
Ravens Roost
Caribbean Cruise Top to Bottom
Arena Stage
Trading Partners (Valentine's Day)
Four Coins
Lower Than the Heart (Valentine's Day)
Brambleton
Gotta Keep Trying
Finding Amnad
Platres Conclave

Other Novels/Novellas

Temptation's Clutches*
Descent into Chaos
Escape to Girne
Journey Through Abilene
Harmony and Dissonance
Stallion Station
Racing With the Devil (espionage suspense)
Cruising Gigolo (bisexual)
Prepared in Cape Verdi
Gilded Cage
House on Park*
Anything for Ambition
Dance of the Ravishers
Hard Knocks U*
My Neighbor's Spa*
Man's Man: Tales of a High Priced Gay Hooker*

Trip Money
The Indian Doctor
Sailorboy
Home to Fire Island
Murder Mysteries
Death on a Ping Pong Table
Clint Folsom Mysteries Compendium Volume 1*
Death to Blonds - Stolen Judgment (Clint Folsom
Mystery)*
Clint Folsom Mysteries Compendium Volume 2*
Gay Erotica Anthologies
Earth Cry*
Shunga
Habu's Christmas Balls
Eight in D*
DevilMENt
Silas' Choices*
Stallion Station (A Novella in Parts)
Eleven to the Dogs*
Fifty Seventy*
Spy Tails 001*
Spy Tails 002*
Doubled*
Doubled Again*
Tails in the Tropics*
Tails in the Med*
Tails in the West*
Rough Riders*
Grab Bag 1*
Grab Bag 2*
Grab Bag 3*
Grab Bag 4*
Grab Bag 5*
Grab Bag 6*
Grab Bag 7*
Beyond the Beaded Curtain*
Habu's Christmas Balls
The Sporting Life*

Gayly Complicated*
Despoiling David
The Tree of Idleness*
I Met a Man
Rough Road to Happiness
BOOKS BY STEPHEN KESSEL
Gay Romance
The Forever Man
Two Chances
BOOKS BY KIM BLACK
Lesbian Romance
Transfixed on Tammie (F/T lesbian)